DEADLY JUSTICE

A GIA SANTELLA CRIME THRILLER
BOOK 14

KRISTI BELCAMINO

LIQUID MIND PUBLISHING

Copyright © 2021 by Kristi Belcamino. All rights reserved. No part of this publication may be copied, reproduced in any format, by any means, electronic or otherwise, without prior consent from the copyright owner and publisher of this book.

Liquid Mind Publishing
This is a work of fiction. All characters, names, places and events are the product of the author's imagination or used fictitiously.

GIA SANTELLA CRIME THRILLER SERIES

Enjoying the Gia Santella series? Scan below to order more books today!

Vendetta

Vigilante

Vengeance

Black Widow

Day of the Dead

Border Line

Night Fall

Stone Cold

Cold as Death

Cold Blooded

Dark Shadows

Dark Vengeance

Dark Justice

Deadly Justice

Deadly Lies

PROLOGUE

My thighs hugged the sides of the bike like it was part of me as I leaned into the curve, my headlight skittering across the steep cliff to my left and then shooting out into the dark night sky as I straightened the bike out.

I quickly glanced into my rearview mirror to see if I could glimpse headlights behind me.

Two vehicles were back there trying to catch up but now the mirror only reflected blackness.

My hands gripped the handles of the bike as I curled into the next bend of the road.

A narrow strip of dusty dirt shoulder on the right was all that separated the roadway—and me—from a deadly plunge to the crashing waves of the Pacific Ocean below.

At some points, the road perched hundreds of feet above the Pacific Ocean on this winding stretch of Pacific Coast Highway between Monterey and Big Sur.

At least once a year some hapless motorist plunges to their death.

When I was young and had just completed the racing course

at Laguna Seca, I used to sneak out at night just to drive this road. I would take the top off my mother's Fiat and crank Metallica as I raced down PCH with my hair blowing in the wind, feeling death at my shoulder and knowing that even the slightest miscalculation would send me plummeting to my death.

I was young and immortal. Living on the edge, pushing the envelope was the only way I knew how to deal with the turmoil of my emotions at the time.

It all seemed so dramatic at the time.

I'd been so clueless.

This was before I was raped.

This was before my parents were murdered.

This was before I'd been forced to become a killer myself.

I'd navigated these curves dozens of times. I had fucking haunted this road in my youth.

Now, there was a glittering in my side mirror and I could see the Porsche SUV headlights coming up fast behind me.

Go ahead and try to take me out here, you bastards.

The Porsche was fast, but it was no match for the crotch rocket between my legs.

It had been a long time and I was a lot older, but I was confident as I took the curves at speeds that caused me to lean so far that my thighs nearly brushed the pavement.

The headlights grew closer.

The sound of gunshots ripped through the night air. Sparks flew off the pavement to my left as I slipped around another corner.

Motherfuckers.

Adrenaline surged through my body.

I knew there was about another mile of curves before the road leveled out for a stretch as it cut through Big Sur.

They might catch up on the straightaways. I wanted to put some ground between us before then., since I had no protection from gunfire on the bike. I was an easy target.

So far, the road had been empty except for me and the two SUV's chasing me.

Everyone else was home tucked into their beds.

In another two hours, the Monterey Peninsula would be busy with vehicles of those who started their work days before the sun rose—the hotel maids, the gardeners and restaurant workers.

All the hardworking people in the service industry who catered to the rich tourists who kept the Peninsula economy flourishing.

But right now the road was ours and ours alone.

The way I figured it, we were about halfway to the flat stretch of the Big Sur town area.

I saw the headlights of the Porsche bouncing off my mirror at the same time I heard gunshots again.

Damn it. I crouched lower on the bike. They were catching up.

One of the trickiest curves was coming up. A hairpin turn with yellow warning signs. I knew I was going much too fast for it. I'd have to slow down. But if I did, the car would be right on my ass. The bullets were coming too close as it was.

Then the hairpin turn was upon me. With my thighs gripping the bike and my hands curled and clenched around the handles of the bike I leaned forward at the same time I eased up on the throttle.

As I did, I was suddenly blinded by the headlights of a huge vehicle rounding the corner before me. In my lane. At the same time, my mirror reflected the headlights of the Porsche, which had caught up to me when I slowed down.

I had about two seconds to decide what to do.

And then realized there was no decision to make.

I laid the bike down.

There was a tremendous metal crunching sound and then everything went black.

1

A WEEK BEFORE

"WELL, THIS IS AWKWARD."

Mayor Anthony Ferraro was a master at understatement.

It was my second date with the mayor of San Francisco. Only because he was so damn persistent. I'd tried to blow him off. For starters, he was Italian. I mean, I was Italian-American, too, but that didn't mean I thought it was a good idea to date another Italian. He was handsome with gorgeous olive skin but looked like he spent his spare time getting mani-pedis. He was just a little "too" pretty and groomed, as if his fancy suits could stand up on their own.

We Italians called men like this, "mammones." They were mama's boys who lived at home, sponging off mama's cooking and cleaning until they were in their forties. Like I said, an Italian man. Better off to avoid them all. They were either mammones or macho pricks.

I liked my men a little more rugged and independent. Like … Ryder.

Despite this, I agreed to go on a moonlight bay cruise with the mayor and was almost pissed to discover that I was actually attracted to him. He was confident, witty, and powerful–qualities I found incredibly sexy and alluring.

So much so that I was eager to get back to my hotel suite and get his pants off.

After a hot and heavy elevator ride up to my hotel suite, we stumbled through the door in a mad embrace only to hear Ryder's voice interrupting us.

I rarely grew flustered, but I could feel my face grow warm.

It got worse as I looked around. The suite was lit with dozens of candles. The sultry sounds of Etta James filled the air.

And then I got a good look at Ryder.

Good god. The man was only wearing a white hotel towel wrapped around his waist.

His hair was longer now, wet and slicked back. A droplet of water still gleamed on his tanned and sleek chest. His tattooed arms rippled with muscles.

For once I was speechless.

The mayor, however, was not.

"I'm guessing it's safe to assume you know this man and he's not a burglar who broke into your room?"

I was snapped out of my silence.

"I do know him. He's not a burglar, but he definitely did break into my room."

"Don't get me wrong," the mayor said, looking at Ryder. "You're a good-looking guy and all, but I'm not really into threesomes. Maybe you should go."

I side eyed the mayor. I'd never seen this side of him—semi-bossy alpha male.

I was debating whether to toss them both out and let them have it out in the hall when Ryder spoke.

"Entirely my fault, bro," Ryder said. "I should've called first."

Bro?

"Do you have a place to stay?" I asked Ryder, ignoring the mayor and his macho posturing.

Ryder didn't live in the states. He lived in the south of France, which made his appearance in my hotel room even more surreal.

Ryder responded by dropping the towel. He was naked. He was quite a specimen—which I already knew, of course.

I saw the mayor's eyes narrow. "I see," he said and raised his eyebrow slightly.

Ryder just winked as he reached for a pile of clothes.

"Oh, stop it," I said. "You two are acting like teenage boys."

I was surprised the mayor didn't whip his cock out to compare.

Ryder tugged on a pair of jeans, sans underwear.

"I can find a place to stay," he said as he pulled on a tight black tee-shirt. "If that's what you really want."

I frowned and bit my lip. I had no idea what I really wanted.

"I think I'm going to call it a night," Anthony said and reached for the door. Then he was gone. I looked around frantically. Fuck.

"Ryder. Stay put. I'll be right back."

I caught up with Anthony right when he punched the down button on the elevator.

"I don't know what to say," I said.

"Well, clearly."

Again, I wasn't sure whether to be impressed by his wit or furious.

"Listen, Ryder lives in France. He's *supposed* to be halfway across the world. I had no idea he was here. I had no idea he was *coming* here. I have no idea how he got into my room, but that's another issue."

The mayor scoffed as the elevator door opened and he stepped inside. I followed him part way.

"Listen. I like you," I said, taking his hands and looking up at him. "I had a different idea on how I wanted this night to end."

I was standing in the door of the elevator. He stuck out a foot on each side to keep the doors from closing.

He surprised me by smiling.

"I had all sorts of ideas. Some I think you might have really liked."

I smiled back.

"I understand if you don't want to see me again—if it's too complicated for you," I said. Because I'm going to be honest, this is nothing. My life is way more complicated in much worse ways than finding a naked guy in my hotel room."

He sighed. "Gia. I already know this. I know you and the life you live are as far from normal and ordinary as anyone I've ever met."

He was right. What else could I say? I opened my mouth to respond but he spoke first.

"That's why you are so damn intriguing. I don't want normal. I don't want ordinary. I want you."

Well, damn.

His eyes bore into me. I stood on tiptoe and looped my arms around his neck. He bowed his head and gave me a long, searing kiss. My body was pressed against his and the elevator doors whooshed shut behind us.

Finally, I drew back and hit the button to open the elevator doors again.

"I'll call you," I said, searching his eyes.

"Will you?"

I didn't answer. I just stood there and watched him as the elevator doors closed. I waited until I saw the elevator heading toward the first floor before I returned to the room.

Back in the room, Ryder was putting on his leather jacket.

"I think I should try this again," he said. "I'll go to the lobby and call you and yell 'surprise' and tell you I'm in town, downstairs actually, and you'll tell me tomorrow would be better and then we meet for breakfast."

I stared at him.

Fuck, he was hot.

He watched my eyes roam his body and a sly smile appeared on his face.

I shook my head no.

"Or," he said, shrugging out of his jacket, "we could just take it from here."

I was on him in two seconds, my mouth on his, my hands feverishly tugging off his jeans and untucking his shirt.

My body knew him so well. And wanted him.

I felt a slight shiver of guilt knowing that I'd just kissed the mayor but that fleeting thought disappeared as he lifted me up and I wrapped my legs around his waist. He swept a stack of books I had piled on the table to the floor and pressed me onto the table, my dress lifted up around my waist. I shut off my brain and let my body take over.

Sex with Ryder consumed me in ways that I both loved and hated at the same time.

I was a fool to think I'd be able to turn him away.

The only way to resist Ryder was to put an ocean or two between us.

Otherwise I was putty in his hands.

2

Ryder and I rarely left my hotel suite for three days.

So what if the staff thought I was eccentric? After all, I owned the hotel now. Well, Dante and I did.

We ordered room service and I only left once or twice on hotel business.

One morning, I had an all-staff meeting to run and was gone for a few hours.

When I got back to the room, Ryder was hunched over a computer.

I came up behind him and kissed the back of his neck. He turned and wrapped his arms around me.

I glanced over his shoulder. My heart sank.

"You're leaving?"

He was looking at flights to France.

"I was commissioned for a job."

Ryder was ex-special forces. His current job was a mixture of security guard and part-time assassin.

He knew my history. I knew his—he was paid to take out people who I secretly hoped were evil. I couldn't stomach the thought of him killing innocents. Plus, it just didn't jive with who he was as a person. So I chose to believe he was "eradicating" scumbags.

"When do you have to leave?" I asked, hating the whining in my voice.

"I'm negotiating that right now."

He closed the laptop. Discussion over.

Knowing our time might be short made every moment with him even more poignant.

We talked late into the night, sharing childhood memories and darker, more haunting reminiscences of the evil we'd both encountered.

He allowed me to talk about the darker side of my life that I usually had to keep tucked deep inside. Even with Nico—who had been a cartel leader and ordered more deaths than I cared to even consider—I hadn't shared this much. Nico had men who did his dirty work. Unlike Nico, I had blood on my hands.

Ryder understood that.

Once, when Ryder was out on my deck smoking, Anthony called.

"Hi," I said, glancing at Ryder's back as he leaned over the rail, the Golden Gate glowing in the sunset beyond him.

"Let me know when we can finish what we started," he said.

I sighed.

"I know, I know," he said. "It's complicated." His voice was sarcastic but also playful.

"Ryder and I have history." It was a lame response. "Loose ends."

"Ryder is such a virile, studly, macho name," Anthony said. "Can't compete with that. But that's not why I called - Of course I want to see you again. Call me when you tie up those loose ends."

I hung up.

Three days later, Anthony called again.

Ryder hadn't mentioned the job back in France and I certainly hadn't brought it up.

I let the mayor's call go to voicemail and then instantly pressed play to listen to it.

"You know," he began, "that people from France can only stay in San Francisco for a total of three days without a special visa issued by the mayor's office. In case you haven't heard of this law, I just passed it this morning. And no, there will not be any visas issued until the next century."

I nearly laughed.

He was persistent as fuck. I'd give him that. He was not put off by the thought that I was basically sleeping with another man. He still wanted me. It was slightly insane.

Ryder watched me as I listened to this message.

He was naked. In my kitchen. Cooking for me.

Looking at him made me smile. His body was perfect.

"At least put an apron on," I said as he sautéed pancetta in olive oil, making it sizzle. "I don't want any part of your body burned."

He laughed. "I cook naked all the time."

I just shook my head.

"That call?" he said. "You look concerned. Your forehead crinkled."

"Oh," I said, thinking that I needed to work on my poker face. "It was the mayor."

"And?" Ryder said, plucking a small piece of cheese off a plate and putting it in his mouth.

"He wants to see me as soon as you leave town."

"And will you?" he asked, turning toward the refrigerator. "See him?"

I waited for a beat and then said, "Would you care?"

He turned back around. "I leave Monday," he said.

I closed my eyes. He'd avoided telling me that he had a plan. My stomach suddenly flip flopped.

"So soon?"

"I was going to tell you tonight," he said.

"You didn't answer my question," I said, leaning my chin onto my fist.

He didn't look at me. He slid the pancetta pasta into two pasta bowls and set them on the table.

"Would you care?" I said again in a soft voice from my spot on the couch.

He walked over, pulled me up, and grabbed my head, kissing me long and hard, his hands tangled in my hair.

"What do you think?" he said in a husky voice as he pulled back.

I stared at him.

"Come with me to France."

"Stay here," I said at nearly the same time.

We both gave strangled laughs.

"You can be a kept man. You don't need to work anymore."

He rolled his eyes and shook his head, but he was smiling.

"Gia, my life is half a world away. Your life is here. Me and you? It is ... impossible ..."

I pulled away. His words hurt more than I'd expected. Walking toward the bedroom I didn't look at him as I spoke.

"I think you need to change your flight and leave tomorrow," I said, trying to keep my voice neutral. "I don't want this to be any harder than it already is." I paused but he didn't say anything so I continued into the bedroom. "I'm staying at Darling's tonight. I'm going to take a shower, pack and then leave. You can stay here tonight."

It hurt but I knew it would hurt more if he stayed another five days. I had to make a clean break right then.

When I got out of the shower, he was gone.

The kitchen was cleaned up. The food was neatly put away under plastic wrap in the refrigerator.

A note on the counter. "Farewell my love."

I wouldn't be packing anything.

Instead I curled up on the couch and stared out the window at my city.

3

THE NEXT MORNING, I CALLED ANTHONY.

"Are you free for breakfast?"

"No, I'm sorry. I'm in San Jose."

Disappointment flooded me.

What did I expect?

"However," Anthony continued. "I was going to call. I heard Pepé Le Pew left town and wanted to see if you were free."

"Maybe. How did you know Ryder was gone again?"

He deftly ignored my question.

"Are you free for the next four days?"

"What?"

"I have a thing in Washington, D.C. It's meeting a bunch of mucky mucks at big fancy parties. It's a last big push—part of my campaign."

Anthony was running for state senator.

The election was in less than three weeks.

"I'd love it if you could be my date," he said.

"Uh..."

"Let me sweeten the pot," he said. "Dante and Wayne will be

there. I'm introducing them to some people. I'll let them explain."

I glanced around my hotel room. Staying here would be depressing without Ryder. And Anthony was really cute and sexy and *he* lived in the same city as me, unlike a certain sexy French man.

"What time are we leaving?"

"Sweeeet!" Anthony said like a little boy and it made me smile. I could imagine him fist pumping.

Two hours later, a limo picked me up at the hotel and drove me to the airport.

Anthony was meeting me there, coming straight from San Jose.

When the limo pulled into the airport, instead of taking me to the terminal, it drove past and headed toward an entrance into a private area.

I wondered if I should be concerned.

But the guard at the gate just waved us through and then I saw a small private jet in front of us. Anthony was standing in front of it in faded jeans, a black dress shirt and sneakers. He had a New York Yankees ball cap pulled low.

He looked surprisingly normal and young.

And hot.

He opened the door for me and grinned.

"Hey," he said.

"Hey?" I said with a question in my voice. "We're flying private?"

"Yeah. So I know this guy…"

"Of course you do."

The limo driver handed him my one small duffel bag.

"You travel light," he said, taking the bag and then passing it to a guy who hurried up the stairs to the jet.

"I wish. Dante sent a bunch of fancy dresses and shoes ahead. He dresses me."

Anthony laughed. "That's right. I almost forgot." He gave me the once over. "He does good. But you look great right now. This might be my favorite Gia look yet."

I didn't respond, but I was secretly pleased.

I'd worn my much loved and worn-in leather pants, my big clunky white Balenciaga Triple S sneakers, and an oversized charcoal gray sweatshirt. My leather pants were surprisingly the most comfortable thing I owned. Way more comfortable than jeans. They were butter soft.

I followed him as he headed toward the stairs leading up to the jet.

Inside, the front few rows were made up of plush swivel seats and then behind them, cushy chairs that recline into beds.

The guy who had taken my duffel bag handed me a drink.

Patrón tequila.

How did he know? I looked at Anthony. Of course.

He was handed a crystal glass with something clear.

It was only eleven in the morning.

"We're not messing around are we?" I said, taking a swig.

"I work hard and party hard. Today I will do both."

"Okay then." I held up my glass. "*Salute!*"

As soon as we were seated, Anthony reached down into his briefcase and took out his laptop.

"I apologize ahead of time. I'm not a good travel companion. I have some work I need to get done before we land."

I reached for my laptop. "Same."

I had a shit ton of tasks to get the hotel up and running. Dante and I were not only remodeling the entire building but also changing the operations. I was in charge of the hotel. Dante was in charge of the restaurant.

Anthony and I were quietly in our own worlds for most of the flight. He swigged another drink and I had two more tequilas.

I kept busy reviewing personnel files of the hotel employees. I wanted to know all the main players in the hotel. I knew most of them, but I wanted to know them even more. I wouldn't micro-manage but I wanted to make sure I had players in place who were so competent I could delegate everything to them. My job would be to promote five people to vice presidents. Each one would oversee a key part of the hotel management. I would put my complete faith and trust in them as a model of perfect delegation. They would have utter autonomy. But I needed to make sure I was putting the right people in place.

When we landed, I stood and stretched, feeling the energy of the city already seeping inside me. A bitter wave of sadness ran over me.

I'd pushed down the reality of what going to D.C. really meant for me and Dante

To me Washington D.C. had Matt's smiling face all over it. Matt was Dante's dead husband.

Matt had been a senator. Matt and my love Bobby, had been murdered within hours of Dante and Matt's wedding ceremony in Positano. A Sicilian mobster with a vendetta against my family had killed them. When Dante had discovered that the murders were connected to my family's sordid history that made the murder of his new husband my fault. It wasn't logical.

He'd eventually forgiven me.

At least I thought he had.

It seemed like a lifetime ago that Dante had invited me to visit D.C. and stay with him and Matt in Matt's condo.

I hadn't been able to go at the time.

I don't think Dante had been back to D.C. since Matt was murdered.

It was good that Dante brought his husband Wayne with him here. It would hopefully allow Dante to create some new memories while still honoring Matt's memory. Wayne was wonderful about Dante's grief, even saying he knows he would've loved Matt if he'd had the chance to meet him.

I was anxious to see how Dante was handling it all.

They were meeting us at the hotel for a drink.

I was suddenly nervous.

I knew that Dante had forgiven me but deep down inside, I also knew that some small part of him would forever blame me for Matt's murder.

4

The hotel's rooftop offered a spectacular view of the White House.

Anthony had walked me to my room after check in and said he'd meet me at the rooftop bar. I'd taken a long shower and realized I was going to be late meeting everyone if I didn't hurry.

With my hair still wavy and damp on my shoulders, I dressed in a backless black halter top, tight black pants and strappy heels with silver studs on them. The outfit made me feel a little femme fatale.

It was perfect. Of course it was—Dante had picked it out.

When I walked into my hotel suite, the clothes Dante had ordered for me had been waiting in my closet. Each one had a note attached telling me when and where to wear it.

The note on this outfit said "Rooftop Bar Drinks."

I walked into the hotel bar to find the three of them laughing uproariously about something. From across the rooftop, I paused to watch. I couldn't help but smile.

Dante was family. I'd do anything for him. And his happiness was more important than my own.

He looked over at me and our eyes met.

For a brief second I searched them for any pain that being in D.C. might have wrought, but all I saw was a sparkle in his eyes.

His brilliant white smile glowing against his olive skin was infectious. It wasn't fair, the older he got the better looking he became. He was small and fit and lithe and his silky black hair swept back from his face like the Italian Stallion he was.

I blew him a kiss and headed over.

The three men stood and we exchanged kisses. I kissed all three of them on the lips.

I kissed Anthony last and as I did, his hand wrapped around my waist and pulled me closer so our kiss was longer. Yummy.

"What's so funny?" I asked when we all sat down.

"Wayne was talking about his niece, Manisha," Dante said. "She just stayed the weekend with us. We let her do our makeup."

Dante pushed his phone over to show me the pictures.

"Oh my God," I said. "You look like the ugliest drag queen I've ever seen."

"Oh hush. He looked hot. Like on fire." Wayne's eyes crinkled in a wide smile. Dante ruffled Wayne's full head of thick blonde hair.

"I mean, the makeup is perfect, but it's just not a good look for you," I said. "How is Manisha? I know how much you guys love children."

The table grew quiet. Wayne and Dante exchanged a look.

I sipped the tequila they had already ordered me and narrowed my eyes. "What aren't you telling me?"

"We've made a decision," Dante said, again giving Wayne a secret smile.

"And?"

"We want to be parents. And we have a question for you. An important one," he said.

I sat back. A question for me?

"Dante, if you would've asked me to sleep with you when we were teenagers, I would've said yes, but at this point in our lives it would totally be incest. You're gonna have to find someone else to make a baby with, even though they won't be nearly as cute as our baby would be."

Dante laughed. "Oh, Gia, we don't want a baby."

"Yeah," Wayne said, haughtily, "We're not sadists. We want a kid who is potty trained and all that. I mean we have a lifestyle to maintain."

Now, I laughed. Wayne had a heart of gold and was also a total diva. He had a personal shopper at Saks Fifth Avenue who sent him thousands of dollars in clothing once a month to try on at home in case he wanted to buy something. He was a super successful businessman and could afford a lavish lifestyle. His outfit today probably cost a grand—Lime green polo shirt with matching belt.

"How soon is all this happening?" I asked.

"That's sort of why we're here," Dante said. "Senator Mitchell has some connection to adopt children in need. Older children who have been lost in the system and need to be placed right away —for the right amount of money. We asked Anthony if he could ask the senator to introduce us and he agreed. We meet with the woman in charge at a party tonight."

"Wow," I said, momentarily at a loss for words. It sounded a bit too good to be true. "Who is Senator Mitchell again? I know he's some big deal here?"

"He's my godfather," Anthony said. "He was a father figure after my own father died growing up. They were colleagues in the early days. He was the one who convinced me to toss my cap in the ring for the senate seat."

His godfather was Senator Mike Mitchell? Interesting. But I was a little concerned about children "lost in the system" being essentially sold.

"Where are these kids found?" I said.

"It's all legal," Dante said, immediately picking up on my skepticism. "It's the same process that someone else would go through except it's speeded up because we can pay more."

"Huh," I said and took a big drink to hide my expression. "What's this party?"

Anthony handed me a thick envelope with my name embossed in gold print on the front.

It contained a thick invitation with gold script and an elaborate gold face mask embossed at the top. I was invited to a masked ball. Gold and black dress. Gold mask required.

"Your dress and mask will be delivered to your room at four," Dante said.

"Damn, you're good," I said.

"Don't you forget it."

So, this was the first fundraising party we'd be attending? Very interesting.

After we finished our drinks, it was time to get ready for the party.

The three men said goodbye when the elevator opened on my floor and it was only as I walked down the hall toward my room that I realized that Wayne had never asked me the "question" he'd mentioned.

Right at eight, Anthony was at my door.

I'd shimmied into the gold silk dress Dante had delivered. It felt like liquid gold on my body, hugging every curve from just above my breasts to just below my knees. He'd sent along strappy gold sandals and a gorgeous gold Mardi gras style mask that only covered my eyes.

Anthony was wearing a black suit with a black dress shirt and a gold tie. He held a plain gold mask in his hand.

He came in and closed the door behind him, locking it.

"I'm not taking you out in the dress."

He undid his tie and flung it on the small table. "We'll just order in. Fuck the fundraiser. I just want to spend the evening looking at you."

His sense of humor sometimes took me off guard. He undid his tie and sprawled on the couch.

"Very funny."

There was another knock on the door. I opened it.

It was Wayne and Dante. They both had on black tuxedos with shiny gold bow ties.

Dante's eyes went from me to Anthony.

"You ready?"

Anthony laughed and stood, reaching for his tie.

"Fine. We'll go to the party," he said.

I ignored the look Dante gave me as I walked past him toward the elevator.

The party was about thirty minutes out of the city at a massive house down a rural lane lined with thick trees. As we pulled onto the lane, a catering truck came careening from the opposite direction and cut us off. Our driver swore and slammed on the brakes.

"Must be late," I said with a shrug.

When we got to the house, I was impressed. It was massive with giant columns and an army of valet parkers racing around parking cars as fast as they could. About a dozen people in black were piling out of the caterer's van. Definitely running late.

We had to give a password at the front door. Anthony said it. The password was "Golden Rod."

I gripped his elbow. "Are you sure about this? With the masks and the house and that password, I'm getting some strong Eyes Wide Shut vibes."

Dante laughed. "You wish."

Anthony raised an eyebrow. "I seemed to have missed that one."

Wayne responded. "It's a Tom Cruise and Nicole Kidman movie - Cruise shows up at this party with all these powerful people in robes and hoods and masks and orgies in every room. A lot of people end up dead."

"I see," Anthony said. "I don't think we will be having orgies here tonight. But I can't say for sure. This is Washington, after all."

Inside the house, we were led to a ballroom filled with men in tuxedos and gold masks and women in gold dresses. The room had a tall arched ceiling topped with a gold dome.

The walls were draped in black velvet and all the furnishings were gold and black.

The large, circular room had several doors leading out of it. Servers in tuxedos and black masks circulated, sometimes bearing aperitifs or glasses of champagne. The food was on gold trays—black caviar sprinkled with gold flakes, gold goblets containing Champagne that had gold flakes floating in it, gold leaf macarons and more.

Anthony introduced me to one important person after the other. I recognize some of them: movie stars, politicians, business moguls.

They all fucking loved him.

The hosts, Senator Wendy Moore and her husband, Camden Moore, were gracious when we met.

"I love the theme," I said. Then I couldn't help it, I cocked my head. "I'm not going to lie, it's a little Eyes Wide Shut."

Senator Moore's laughter rang out and a few heads turned.

"My little secret is out. I do adore that movie."

"Is there another room for the orgies?" I innocently asked, taking a sip of my Champagne.

Camden Moore actually flushed red. But he recovered quickly.

"I don't know," he said, turning to his wife. "Is there, my dear?"

"I'm afraid not, Cam," she said. "I was saving that for my fiftieth birthday party next year."

"Oh goodie," I said. "Will I be invited?"

"Oh darling," she said. "You will be my special guest."

Now, I flushed.

Senator Moore played for both teams. Or did she?

I didn't. Or at least I hadn't up to that point in my life.

And frankly, while the senator was a gorgeous woman, I wasn't in the least tempted to start on a new team right then. I had enough problems with my current roster.

Someone called her name and she gave me a slow wink. "I must run."

Then they were gone.

"Whoa."

Anthony laughed. "She's a force of nature."

"I'll say."

"When she backs someone's campaign, she brings half the senate with her."

"Nice," I said.

After a pause I said, "Do I have to sleep with her to get her to support you or do you have to sleep with her or do both of us at the same time?"

Again, he laughed. "I like where your head's at, Sport. But no. She's already pledged her support and I didn't even have to sleep with her. Luckily, she's very strict at keeping business separate from pleasure."

"Phew. That's a relief."

"Aha, here comes my master," Anthony said with a bite to his voice. "Allow me to introduce you to Senator Mitchell."

This is why we were here. This powerful politician.

I straightened.

According to Anthony, being aligned with Senator Mitchell would be the difference between getting elected or not. It seemed so rigged. He hadn't really spoken bad about the senator, but had mentioned on the plane that he wasn't exactly thrilled he'd been ordered to D.C. for these parties.

The Senator was handsome in a generic way. He had a full head of dark blonde hair and had a bit of a Robert Redford vibe. Very masculine. He had a ready grin and a firm handshake. His dark brown eyes held something less friendly than his smile, though. I couldn't figure out what it was.

He dipped his head and kissed the back of my hand. I didn't react.

"Anthony tells me you grew up on the Monterey Peninsula?"

"I did," I said and gulped down my Champagne.

He cocked his head. "Santella? I'm pretty sure I did business with your father back in the day when I first bought my house in Carmel."

I smiled. "Maybe. He did know everyone."

I missed my daddy so bad my gut ached simply talking about him after all these years.

"We used to have meetings at one of the old sardine factories," he said. "I'd always leave with massive bundles of fresh fish. My family would eat well for weeks."

I smiled wider. "That was my dad for sure," I said. "He never let someone leave a meeting without some sort of gift like that."

As we exchanged banalities about how much the Monterey Peninsula had changed in the past fifteen years, I tried to put my finger on what it was about him that was unsettling.

He walked the walk. He was charming, polite, intelligent, good at directing the attention to the person he was speaking to. In other words, he was the quintessential politician who would go a long way up the ladder.

He exuded power.

It was only when Anthony brought up some bill to help immigrants that I saw a flash of something incongruent. It was that darkness in his eyes again that was a disconnect from that easy grin.

Instead of answering Anthony, he turned to me.

"May I borrow Anthony for a moment? We have some business to discuss that I'm sure will bore you."

"I'm sure." I said.

Then they were gone.

Despite his nearly flawless performance, I didn't like Senator Mitchell. He felt slimy.

Then it hit me what felt off about him.

It was one word that described how he made me feel and summed up the vibe he gave off:

Predatory.

5

THEY LEFT ME AND I STOOD ALONE ALONG THE FAR WALL, scanning the crowd when I noticed a slim young woman with long brown hair come stand beside me, pressing her back to the wall, as well. She was shifting from foot to foot.

I smiled at her, glad my mask only covered my eyes.

She smiled back. But she seemed nervous. She was holding her champagne flute with one hand and cracking the knuckles of her fingers on the other. It made her seem so young and vulnerable. My heart went out to her. I turned and smiled.

"Hi, I'm Gia," I said.

"I'm Meg."

"Quite a party," I said.

"Yeah," she said with a nervous giggle. "We don't have parties like this back in Des Moines."

I laughed. "We don't have them like this in San Francisco, either. At least not ones I've ever been invited to."

"You live in San Francisco?" she said. "I get to go there for the first time next week."

"Oh yeah?"

"I'm an intern for Senator Mitchell," she said. Her voice

sounded both embarrassed and proud. "When I started the school year I had no idea he was going to be a presidential candidate. So now I get to go on the campaign trail with him. We'll be in California next week."

"What's it like working for him?"

I thought about how he had been both charismatic and pervy at the same time. And how, despite the high gloss image he presented, he seemed slimy.

"He's really smart and charismatic and is going to make some big changes in this country. He's already done a lot," her eyes were shining with passion.

Damn girl had it bad.

"Does he treat you well? I mean is he a good boss? Sometimes men can be such pricks to young women who work for them."

"He's a total gentleman," she said. "He is very respectful. He tells me I don't have to work late even though I like to do it. When we work late nights, he always has his own personal driver take me home. And he always orders expensive take out for everyone in the office. He won't even let me pay for my own coffee. He also gives me a clothing allowance for events like this. He says he wants me to feel comfortable and fit in."

I bet he does. I decided to change the subject. There's nothing I can say to this young woman to warn her. After all, I just had a gut feeling about the guy. Plus, she's clearly already drunk the Kool-Aid.

"Do you think his re-election will make a difference? Is there a reason he hasn't been able to do some of this stuff already during his current term?" I asked.

I wasn't being difficult. I was genuinely curious. I'd never been big into politics. I usually just voted party line and hoped for the best.

She was about to answer when a woman with a severe gray haircut waved at her.

"That's Julia, the campaign manager. I better go."

"Good luck," I said after her, but she had scurried away.

I was scanning the room for Dante and Wayne when a man in a mask made a beeline toward me.

I began to walk toward Dante and Wayne, deftly sidestepping the man heading my way.

The blonde woman they were speaking to wore a gold lamé dress that grazed her curvy backside and then dipped low in the front showing impressive cleavage. Her face was cherubic but she was probably in her fifties. Her blonde hair was nearly the same color as her dress. She was what Marilyn Monroe would have probably looked like had she lived to be fifty.

Dante and Wayne were bent over listening intently to whatever she was saying.

I was intrigued. I made my way through the crowd toward them leaving the burly man standing there with his mouth open.

When I arrived, Dante slightly jerked back from the woman as if he were guilty of something.

The woman, who had been talking, didn't turn to look at me as I joined their circle.

"Katiana? This is Gia Santella," Dante said.

The woman turned and cocked her head. "Welcome," she said, as if she were hosting the party.

I smiled.

"The pleasure is mine," I said and drained my glass. Dante gave me a look. He and Wayne didn't drink and judged the fuck out of me for enjoying my booze.

"Jonathan," she said loudly. One of the servers in the black mask and tuxedo turned.

"Will you please get Miss Santella a new drink?"

"Thank you so much," I said with a smile directed at Dante.

"Of course," she said and then reached to touch Dante's arm. "Until tomorrow then," she told him. Then she drifted away, leaving a cloud of cloying perfume in her wake.

"What's up with Blondie?" I asked.

Dante and Wayne couldn't wait to tell me. Katiana was the one who "procured" the children that the one percenters adopted.

"Procured sounds sort of fucked up," I said and took a long sip of the Champagne glass the waiter had handed me. Damn he was fast.

"It's a nice way of saying she arranged the adoption. I mean she could use the word 'rescues' as well."

I squinted. "Where again does she 'rescue' these kids?"

"It has to be a little on the down low because these are kids whose parents have abused them. They would otherwise be thrown into the foster system, which we all know is ripe with abuse, people trying to make a buck, or they can be adopted by people like us with money."

"Huh," I said. I was suddenly flushed and felt a little dizzy. "How do they help these kids with all the issues they might have from, say, being abused?"

"That's what's so amazing," Wayne said. "They are assigned therapists from the minute they come into the system and that therapist stays with them for the long haul."

"Cool," I said. But I still was wary. It sounded too good to be true. I was burning up all of a sudden. All the booze and the crowded room was getting to me.

"She showed us pictures of two possible children who will be coming up for adoption soon," Dante said. "Gia, this is so important to me. I hope you understand and support this even if it seems a little odd. It has to be kept quiet because it is unconventional."

Of course Dante had picked up on my reservations about it.

I gave him a tight smile. I was feeling really drunk.

I scanned the room for Anthony, but it was crowded and I couldn't see his dark head.

"I'm going outside to smoke," I said and walked away.

As I made my way through the crowd, I spotted Blondie again. She had her hand on the elbow of a young woman. The woman had curly brown hair and was tall and gangly like a colt with too long legs. What stood out to me the most was that she wore a white minidress—she wasn't wearing gold. Or a mask. Her eyes were unfocused. Was she drunk? Or drugged. She did stumble a little.

Even from a few feet away, I could see Blondie's nails digging into the woman's arm, turning the skin around it white. What the hell?

The younger woman seemed meek, however, not fighting and allowing herself to be steered toward the door they were heading for.

Blondie opened the door and the two women disappeared inside.

I waited a beat and then walked over to the door, trying the handle. It was locked. I looked up. There was a small camera above it. Interesting.

The room swam before me. Fuck. How many drinks had I had? I thought three or four? That was nothing for me. Did gold-flaked Champagne fuck you up easier?

I found the door leading to a deck and joined a few people who were outside smoking.

A woman dressed in a black maid's outfit with a gold apron was carrying a tray of bacon dipped in chocolate and sprinkled with gold flakes. She stopped to offer me one.

I started to reach for one, but felt a wave of nausea.

"No thank you. But I have a question," I said.

She paused.

"Where do all the doors leading from the main ballroom go to? My friend went inside one and when I went to follow it was locked."

The woman looked around in both directions before she answered.

Her voice was low. "We were told not to go into any of the other rooms. They are strictly off limits."

"Really?" I said. "Why's that?"

She shrugged. "We were told that if we saw anything 'interesting' to ignore it or we wouldn't be paid."

"What do you mean by interesting?" I said leaning closer.

"Any strange noises or things."

"Noises?"

She nodded. "Yes."

"Did you hear any strange noises tonight?"

She nodded again.

"What did you hear?"

She looked around again. The couple at the end of the rail had gone inside. We were alone.

"What?" My voice was louder than I'd intended. "What did you hear?"

A group came outside. A man in a tuxedo carrying a tray of Champagne headed straight for us. "Marta? You're wanted in the kitchen."

She left without another word. Marta. I made note of her name.

The man offered me a glass of Champagne and I took it. He lingered for a minute too long. What the fuck? Had they heard or seen me questioning Marta and sent someone to interrupt? It sure as hell seemed that way.

I wandered back inside.

Anthony was talking to a beautiful woman with red hair. He

was leaning down to hear her and she had her hand on his sleeve. She had long pointed gold painted nails.

I knew I should feel jealous but I didn't.

At that moment, I saw Katiana again. She was steering a gray-haired senator I'd met earlier toward the same door where she'd disappeared with the curly-haired woman earlier. I made my way through the crowd in time to see the door open. But when I looked through the open doorway, all I saw was black. Katiana and the man were inside within seconds and the door closed behind them.

I was determined to stay near the door until Katiana and the man came back out, but before I could stake a claim, Anthony was at my side. Apparently, he'd been able to ditch the redhead.

"What's back there?" I said and jutted my chin at the closed door.

"Good question."

"That's not an answer."

"I presume the living quarters."

"What's that mean?" I was irritated with his vague answers.

He shrugged. "Bedrooms."

"Oh."

"Yes."

"So young women and old men keep getting escorted back there for a reason?" I asked.

"It's not the face politicians like to present to the world but yes," he said. "Your guess is probably accurate."

I looked around. I saw the woman with the red hair whispering into the ear of another man, her gold taloned nails now on his sleeve.

"That's pretty fucked up."

"That's D.C for you."

"Fuck me."

He laughed. "It's the way it works in any place in the world where there is power and wealth, Gia," he said. "Don't tell me this surprises you."

"No, it doesn't. I just usually try to avoid parties like these."

Then I felt Anthony's hand on the small of my back. He steered me away from the door and toward the balcony. Once out there, he took my hand and led me to the dark far corner and there he lifted my chin and kissed me long and hard.

"I've been wanting to do that all night."

"Me too," I said.

Just then there was a commotion inside. A woman screamed and there were raised voices.

We rushed inside with the others.

"What happened?" Anthony said to a man he apparently knew.

"There's been an accident. A woman is dead."

6

It was Eyes Wide Shut.

Sort of.

After the death had been discovered, the party ended.

We were all escorted out front where we all stood in a huddle waiting in line as valets rushed to bring forth cars. Three police cars and two ambulances arrived. Sirens and lights off.

Anthony walked over and was speaking to Senator Moore. She removed her mask to greet the police officers as they came up the stairs.

Anthony came back over to our group.

"Who was it? How did she die?" I asked.

"From what I heard, it appears she overdosed."

"Just like in the movie!" I said loudly.

"Gia," Dante said. His voice held a warning.

"Who was she?" I repeated.

"She was hired to be here. A prostitute," Anthony said simply. "As I said, unfortunately, it's the way things work here."

"Oh crap," I said suddenly. "I forgot something inside."

I turned and slipped back in the door before anyone could stop me.

I heard Senator Moore protest but I was already gone.

I headed straight toward the ballroom and then toward the door that I'd seen Blondie disappear into. It was unlocked. I opened it and saw a long hallway. There were voices coming from an open door down the hall. A strip of light from the open door fell across the thick rug.

I saw a shadow and dipped into an open doorway to my right. The room was dark. I held my breath as I heard more commotion and the voices became louder.

They were coming this way.

"Get that door," a deep voice said.

"Shit, she almost slipped off the gurney," someone else said.

"I told you to find something to cover her face and head."

"Relax. Nobody is going to see her neck. We won't let anyone that close. You can barely see any marks."

"Dude. I told you to cover it the fuck up."

At this point, they were right at the doorway, a few feet away from me.

I shrank a bit back into the dark room.

They paused in front of the door leading into the ballroom.

"I'm not going out there until you cover her face."

The guy at the front of the gurney passed me and stopped. That meant the woman on the gurney's head was right in front of me, facing me. Of course the first place I looked was her neck. there were faint red marks on the pale flesh. The one guy was right. Even a few feet away they were hard to see. Her eyes were wide open and lifeless.

"Here," a man said. A second later, a white cloth napkin was draped over her face.

Then the door opened and they were gone. I sensed rather than heard I still wasn't alone.

As soon as the door clicked shut, I heard voices.

One was Blondie.

"I can't let this ever happen again," she said lightly.

"I don't think you should take that tone with me," a man's voice said.

"If you like my services, I suggest you try your best not to jeopardize my business again."

"Oh honey, nothing is jeopardized. Don't you know I own this town?"

Then they were in front of me. I froze.

It was Senator Mitchell.

"I hope you're right," Blondie said.

Then the door opened and they were both gone. I swayed in the dark feeling woozy and drunker than I'd been in a long time.

I waited a few beats and then stepped out of my dark room and pressed my ear to the outside door to the ballroom.

I didn't hear anything so very slowly I cracked the door and peeked out

The ballroom was empty. As quickly as I could, I stepped out and closed the door behind me and walked toward the door leading to the balcony.

I pretended to search near a flower pot and was glad I did because a few seconds later Senator Moore appeared.

"Did you find what you were looking for?"

I frowned. "No. It's a silver cigarette case. Vintage with sentimental value."

Fuck, my voice was slurred.

"Oh dear, that's too bad."

Something about her tone sent an alarm through me. She wasn't buying my story.

"Could I give you my number in case one of the staff already found it or finds it later?"

She gave a tight smile. "I know how to get a hold of you."

"Thanks." I brushed past her. I knew I was walking crooked, holding the wall for balance.

"You know,' she said as I walked away. "You can remove your mask now."

I ignored her and walked as fast as I could toward the front door.

Anthony was off to one side waiting for me. The police cars and ambulance were already gone.

I knew enough about homicide investigations to know that there was no way in hell the cops were done with a death investigation. Not in a million years. Something was royally fucked up at this place. I kept my opinion to myself and gave Anthony a bright smile.

"Hello, sailor," I said in a sultry voice.

"Dante and Wayne are already in the car,' he said. "Did you find what you were looking for?"

"Long story but I've lost my cigarette case."

"Oh no."

Fortunately, Wayne and Dante's chatter about adoption took up most of the conversation on the ride back to the city. I was so drunk that I just sat there silently with my head on Anthony's shoulder.

I wasn't ready to share what I'd seen and heard yet. My mind was still reeling. I was drunk but I knew what I'd seen and heard.

The senator had killed a woman. And Blondie was covering it up.

It was fucked on so many levels.

I dreaded what this all meant for Dante and Wayne.

They were so fucking excited about adoption.

Anthony put his hand on my thigh in the dark and I didn't move it.

We all rode up in the hotel elevator together. Dante and Wayne got out of the elevator at their floor first.

When it got to my floor, Anthony moved so he was standing right in front of me. "I can escort you to your room."

"I'm good," I said and stepped out unsteadily. I didn't explain. I needed to sober up and think about what I'd seen and decide what to do about it. If I said something now, fucked up, nobody would believe me.

His eyes scanned my face for a second and then he leaned over and his lips brushed my cheek right before I stepped out of the elevator.

As I stripped off my clothes and got ready for bed, I realized I was really fucked up.

I was brushing my teeth when it hit and then I was vomiting until I dry heaved.

It wasn't like me. I laid down on the bathroom floor. What the fuck?

As I lay there I kept thinking about the dead woman I'd seen.

Anthony's godfather killed her.

I didn't know Anthony that well. Was he everything he seemed?

The simple fact was that he was closely aligned with the senator.

His mentor was a cold-blooded killer.

Fuck. Just when I thought I'd met a nice guy.

7

THE NEXT MORNING, I WOKE UP WITH A RAGING HEADACHE. I'D managed to drag myself to bed and slept for ten hours straight. I still felt sort of shitty when I woke.

I ordered room service coffee and then took out my laptop. I scanned all the news sites in Washington for word about the woman's overdose. Not a word.

Even the murder in "Eyes Wide Shut" had been reported in the paper as an overdose.

But there was no mention of any of it.

I called Dante but his phone went to voicemail.

Reluctantly, I called Anthony.

"There's nothing in the paper about that woman dying last night."

"It's an overdose of a prostitute. Not to be insensitive, but I hardly think it's newsworthy."

You're not helping your case, I thought.

"Is that how you would respond as a mayor or as a human being?" I asked, testing the waters.

"I'd like to think it's the same thing."

I didn't answer.

"Listen, I know it's weird. I know it's fucked up," he gave a loud sigh. "But that's how they operate in D.C. There is a whole business model where people have been made into millionaires by perfecting how to hide crimes and avoid scandals."

"You sound really concerned," I said.

"I guess I assumed you knew how I really feel. I mean you know my platform, right? I'm all about funding programs to reduce homelessness, fund programs to help addictions, and give women other options besides prostitution. It's just that this is not my city. I have to accept how fucked up it is here until I'm elected in some capacity to make a difference."

A trickle of relief flooded me. This was the man I knew.

His casual talk about how things are handled in D.C. didn't mean he approved.

There was a long pause as I mulled all this over.

"What if you are condoning this behavior without even realizing it simply because you are aligned with people that condone it?" I asked.

"Are you saying the senator condones it? I don't think so. He sent out an email this morning saying he was mortified that the death had occurred and was contacting the woman's family and making a large donation for her funeral expenses and a memorial."

That fucker.

"What if it wasn't an overdose? What if someone killed her? What if the senator killed her? Then what?"

Again, I was testing the waters. I wanted to see how much Anthony knew.

"Jesus Christ. Do you think I would ever be associated with someone like that? He's my godfather. I've known him my whole life."

I closed my eyes. I really, really wanted to tell him. But I didn't entirely trust him.

When I didn't answer, he kept talking.

"Gia, I know. I know it's heartless and fucked up. I'm not saying I approve. I'm saying that this makes it even more important that I get elected. And if it means I have to keep my nose down until I'm in a place where I can do something about it, then that's what I have to do. Believe me I wish it wasn't that way."

"Anthony, that sounds great, but I just wonder if the ante doesn't get higher the more you move up into positions of power. I mean, unless you're the president, you're always going to be under someone else's thumb, right?"

He was silent for a moment.

"I truly hope not."

My phone beeped. I glanced down and read it.

"It's Dante," I told Anthony. "He wants to go grab a coffee at a 'sweet' little spot nearby," I read. "You in?"

"I'm in, baby. Meet you downstairs in ten."

I was relieved that instead of hopping in another limo, we walked two blocks to a breakfast place where we could sit in the back courtyard surrounded by flowers and plants. The decor was art deco and there was a gorgeous fountain with a stunning nude in the center. It was a perfect oasis from the bustling city street out front.

It was lovely. They served one of the best lattes I'd ever had and my standards were high after living in the Italian section of San Francisco.

They served petit fours and flaky croissants and scones.

"I don't care if I ever eat another gold-flaked cupcake again," Wayne said, patting his stomach.

"Did you get sick too?" I asked.

Dante rolled his eyes. "You got sick because you drank too much, Gia."

I glared at him. "Bullshit. I ate something bad."

But I didn't even believe myself.

I side-eyed Anthony to see his reaction but he was just stuffing his face with food.

"You were right," he said to Dante. "This is a sweet little place."

The only thing that wasn't sweet was the apprehension and unease I felt sitting there with Anthony when I knew that his mentor/father figure was a killer and it would be up to me to prove it if I was going to get him to distance himself from the senator.

Because I'd decided unless I had proof, I was just going to alienate Anthony. He apparently thought the sun rose and set over that fucker.

Wayne was telling a funny story about one of his clients when his phone dinged.

He looked down and gasped.

"She's beautiful!"

Dante leaned over and his eyes widened and he grabbed his heart.

"She's perfect."

I gave Anthony a look and he raised his eyebrow.

Wayne pushed his phone across the table to us.

"Katiana just sent us pictures of a girl who just became available for adoption."

Dante beamed. "We're going to lunch to meet a couple who adopted their daughter through Katiana so they can talk about their experience."

"Are you sure," I said. I didn't hide my wariness.

"Gia, remember these are children who are suffering waiting for their forever home," Dante said. "Katiana is able to get them settled into families sooner. These children are rescued from awful situations. They need special services that money can buy—services that they won't get if they are stuck in a foster home for months."

"That makes sense, but it just sounds," I paused, struggling for the word, "maybe too perfect?"

Dante stood. I could tell I'd pissed him off.

"We better run. I'm going to swing by the gourmet market at the hotel and put together a gift basket for the couple we're meeting. I've already paid the bill." He leaned down and kissed me goodbye.

Then they were gone.

I scanned my phone for any news of the overdose.

"Nothing about the dead woman," I said and looked up at Anthony to see his reaction.

Anthony met my eyes.

"There won't be anything. It was just an overdose, Gia."

"Was it?"

For a second I was tempted to tell him what I'd seen and heard, but the truth was I didn't entirely trust Anthony. Not yet.

I'd thought I knew who he was. But he was so closely aligned with Senator Mitchell, that I couldn't be sure anymore.

"This Katiana?" I said. "Your godfather wouldn't recommend anyone hinky would he?"

"I would be very surprised," he said. "I've known him my whole life."

I bit my lip. There was nothing I could say.

But I could feel that my question had created a distance between us.

He walked me back to the hotel lobby and said he'd meet me later for dinner, that he had lunch with a donor.

I decided to take the stairs to the eighth floor to get in a little exercise.

As I walked up, I ran over everything that had happened at the party last night.

And that's when I remembered what that server, Marta, had said: "The staff had been instructed to ignore any noises they heard."

8

Time to talk to Marta.

I called Anthony to ask for Senator Moore's phone number on the pretext that I was checking about my silver cigarette case.

Before he gave me the number he apologized that he had to cancel dinner with me.

"I'm being introduced to some other donors. This is the final push for the election and we apparently need more money to pay for some TV ads."

"It's fine," I said, actually relieved to have time to look into what had happened to the dead woman.

Anthony reeled off the number and as I wrote it down, I saw my silver cigarette case sticking out of my duffel bag. I moved over to punch it down under some clothes.

Senator Moore picked up right away. Anthony must have her personal cell.

"I'm sorry to bother you," I said. "I was wondering if anyone had found my case. It's silly because it's not worth anything besides sentimental value."

"Not silly at all," she answered in a crisp, brisk voice. "Some things are priceless."

I heard some people in the background talking.

"I'm about to start a meeting so I must go, but I can say that unfortunately, nobody has come forward with your case."

Of course they haven't.

"Damn,"

"I'll call you if it turns up."

"Wait," I said quickly before she hung up. "The last time I saw it was out on the patio when one of the servers was giving me a drink. I'm sure you hired the best caterers out there and it is unlikely anyone would steal it, but could I get the catering company's phone number and just check. At least then I'll feel I've done everything."

There was such a long pause that I wondered if she was on to my game.

Finally, she spouted out a number. The interaction was decidedly chillier.

Red flag.

"Good luck."

And then she hung up.

I texted my pal Danny. He was a millennial. We never spoke on the phone.

Danny was a world-class hacker. He'd become emancipated at seventeen—with my help—because of a fucked-up home life. He'd saved my butt more times than I could count.

He'd been living with—and successfully fighting—a disease that some called Gigantism. It made him grow too much too fast. I hated to think about it because most people with it died young.

He was a little socially awkward unless he was talking about tech stuff but was a rock-solid, good guy with a heart of gold. I'd take a bullet for him without blinking.

"I need an address for a woman named Marta who works for this company," I wrote.

"Give me ten minutes," he texted back.

I loved Danny. While I waited for him to get back to me. I stalked Dante on Snapmap. It looked like he wasn't far from the hotel in a car. His lunch meeting must have been short.

I dialed his number.

"I want to talk to you about Blondie," I said. "In private. Without Anthony around."

"Her name is Katiana."

I ignored him.

"That woman who died at the party? She was murdered."

"What are you talking about? You're still on that?"

I bristled. *On that?*

"Dante, I heard Blondie and the Senator talking. He killed her. Blondie is helping him cover it up. I saw the body. She was strangled."

"Gia, that's impossible."

"I heard it. I saw it."

"Gia, you've been under a lot of stress lately. I think the idea of me and Wayne adopting triggered something in you. Not to mention you were extremely drunk."

"I have no fucking idea what you are talking about."

"Gia."

The way he said it made me pause. I didn't argue about being drunk but said, "Explain how that would trigger me."

"You don't remember?"

"Remember what?" I reached for my cigarette case and lit one even though I was in a non-smoking room. I realized my hand was shaking.

"You and Bobby."

I froze. There was a flicker of something. Some memory. We were standing on the balcony in Positano before Dante's wedding. Holy fuck.

We talked about adopting. A child.

We'd seen a homeless mother and her children in front of a church earlier that day.

"I've always dreamed of adoption," Bobby had told me.

I was surprised by his comment.

"Do you want kids?" he asked.

I remember thinking "Whoa, slow down, sailor," but then I looked over at his face and nodded.

I didn't tell him I hadn't wanted kids. But with Bobby as a father? It suddenly seemed like my destiny.

"I'd like to start with an older kid who is in need," he said.

I looked at him and thought I'd never loved him more.

Then Bobby's phone rang. He put it on speaker phone as he answered. It was Dante.

"Where's my best man?"

"We're leaving here in a few minutes. I just convinced Gia we should adopt a kid in need. Maybe a little girl who is seven or eight?"

"Brilliant," Dante said. "Now get your tight little ass over here. I need a best man for this wedding. Matt insisted we do the traditional thing. And I need my best friend to walk me down the aisle, or the beach or whatever it is."

"We're leaving in two minutes," I'd said.

Before the night ended Bobby would be dead and Matt would be fighting to stay alive in the hospital. He lost that fight.

Now, in Washington, D.C., this conversation came back to me. I'd tucked it deep away with all the horrific memories of that night.

I swallowed the lump in my throat.

"That's not what this is about."

"Gia, I remember that right after Bobby's death you did have some weird stuff happen. Maybe us adopting triggered that PTSD stuff."

With horror, I remembered that right after the murders, once I'd taken the life of the man who took Bobby and Matt away, I fell into a deep dark abyss where I did have hallucinations. I felt like everyone everywhere was trying to kill me and Dante.

I'd checked into a mental health unit at the hospital for two weeks.

Somehow, I'd blocked all that out as well.

"Why do you think it's the same?" I said.

"Katiana was outside talking to Wayne and I when you came outside, remember?"

"No," I said, blinking. "When I came out you guys were already in the car?"

Or were they?

"Gia, you were really inebriated. I don't remember you being that drunk in a really long time."

"I don't understand," I said. "I only had three drinks. Maybe four at the most."

I was proud of my ability to hold my liquor. Three drinks were nothing. Nothing.

"Gia, I think you need help."

"Dante, I know what I saw. I know what I heard."

"Listen, I have to go."

He hung up. I stared at my phone for a few seconds.

What the fuck?

While we'd been talking, Danny had texted me.

"Nobody named Marta works there. And I hacked into their system. they didn't work at your fancy party."

Senator Wendy Moore had lied to me. Why?

I wasn't sure what to do.

Then, I remembered. The catering van that had pulled out and nearly hit our car when we arrived. Then I'd seen it again up by the house.

I closed my eyes. *Think, Gia. What did you see?* It was before I started drinking.

In my mind's eye, I saw some big black curvy type but I couldn't make out the name.

Fuck. But there was a logo.

That came back to me.

It was an illustrated picture of a sexy woman in an apron with one high-heel kicked up behind her, holding a covered plate. It was black on red.

I grabbed my phone and googled Washington, D.C. catering company logos and hit images.

I scrolled through them. It wasn't until the third page that I found it.

Bingo.

Haute Mama catering company.

I quickly texted Danny the name.

"Stand by."

Within five minutes he had sent me an address for Marta.

I looked at the map. The address in the suburbs south of here.

I ordered a car and headed downstairs.

I wasn't imagining things. I wasn't drunk and I wasn't hallucinating. I'd seen that woman's neck and I'd heard Blondie and Senator Mitchell talking.

Senator Mitchell had murdered that woman. That woman deserved justice.

And I'd make sure she got it.

Even if nobody else believed me.

9

The taxi stopped in front of Marta's apartment building in Anacostia. The neighborhood was billed as historic and lay right across from the Frederick Douglass Bridge.

The neighborhood didn't look dangerous but it also was far from any main streets so I paid the taxi driver to wait for me.

The building looked like it housed about a hundred apartments and was a three-story red-brick blocky structure. A dead yellowed lawn surrounded it. It didn't look very historic.

The glass front door looked like it was supposed to be kept closed and locked but was slightly ajar.

I went in and scanned the names on the mailboxes.

Marta Rodriguez was in apartment 202.

I took the stairs.

The stairs were wooden and creaked loudly as I scaled them. A woman on the first floor cracked her door and peeked out at me through the opening the chain allowed.

"Good morning," I said cheerily.

The door instantly slammed shut.

On the second floor, I saw the room I wanted at the far end of the hall. As I made my way toward it, I inhaled deeply.

The hall smelled good, like someone was frying something spicy and delicious for dinner. I heard rap music blaring from one doorway as I made my way down the hall to Unit 202. When I passed another door, I heard the sounds of a talk show.

Then I was in front of Unit 202. I paused listening to see if I could hear anything coming out of that apartment. I caught the faint sounds of Cuban music. It sounded like something you'd want to listen to on a Caribbean island with a frothy cocktail in your hand.

I rapped on the door and waited.

The music turned off. I listened to see if I could hear footsteps approaching the door, but it was eerily silent inside the apartment.

I shifted from one foot to the other, wishing I hadn't worn my high-heel ankle boots. I could run and fight in them but suddenly I wished I'd worn my flat steel-toed combat boots. I wasn't sure why. This neighborhood seemed safe enough. This apartment building was probably fine. I wasn't sure why a trickle of apprehension rolled down my spine.

I knocked again, harder this time. This time I still didn't hear anything but I sensed someone on the other side of the door and then I audibly heard a loud sigh.

"Marta? I was at the party the other night. I lost my cigarette case there and wanted to ask you about it."

I stuck to the same ruse.

The door flung open and there was Marta standing there wearing a neat blue shift with a flowered apron over it. She took me in with her flour-coated hands on her hips.

"You think because I am Latina that I took your stupid cigarette case? You are a crazy bitch."

I was so stunned I didn't answer at first. And then I laughed out loud.

"No," I said adamantly. "No fucking way I think that. I was just trying to get you to open the door."

Her eyes, thickly lined in black kohl, narrowed dangerously. I mentally braced for that flour-coated palm to attempt to slap me.

"I'm here because you and I both know that girl was murdered and didn't overdose," I said. "I need your help. They are saying I'm crazy and that I imagined seeing her with strangle marks on her neck and hearing her killer confess.

"I never seen you before in my life, miss," she said and started to close the door. She wouldn't meet my eyes.

I stuck the toe of my boot between the door and the jamb.

"Bullshit," I said. "You told me about the noises. About ignoring the noises."

She shook her head.

"Wasn't me."

"Why are you lying? Nobody can hear us. It's just me here. I won't tell anyone what you say. I just need information from you to point me in the right direction. I want to know who you saw go in that room and what you might have seen."

She didn't answer and it gave me hope.

"I can give you a reward for the information," I said to try another tact.

She made a loud scoffing sound. "Pffttt," she said. "Reward? You get me a new job, maybe a few bucks? You think that will protect me? You have no idea."

"Tell me," I begged.

"Leave now or I'll call the police."

"Maybe you should and we can have a conversation with them about what you saw and heard?"

She laughed so hard I was taken aback.

"Your first mistake is thinking the police will help. They do what he says. You know nothing."

"Please just point me in the right direction," I said. "Who is behind all this?"

"I never see you in my life. I don't even know what you are talking about. You are crazy lady who comes to my house and won't let me close the door. Now I will scream."

And to my astonishment, that's exactly what she did.

She opened her mouth and screamed bloody murder.

Then we both stood there and stared at one another for a few seconds.

The door across the hall slammed open and I found myself pressed against the wall, a beefy forearm against my neck.

"What's the problem?" my assailant growled.

It was a big, muscled man with a hairy, tattooed arm and bristly beard and beer breath.

Fuck.

"I thought she was somebody else," I said. "It's a case of mistaken identity. I'm leaving now."

He didn't loosen the pressure on my neck.

"Is that true?" he asked Marta.

"*Si*," she said. "Dumb bitch thinks all Latina women look the same. She is looking for someone named Maria. Not Marta."

I shot her a grateful look.

He glared at me for a second, but the pressure eased.

"I'll make sure she leaves and doesn't come back," he said.

"Thank you, Luis."

"Anytime, Ms. Rodriguez."

Then he had an arm looped around my neck and was herding me toward the stairs.

"Ease off, sailor," I said. "I can let myself out."

"I don't think so," he said.

But I easily wriggled out of his grasp and was halfway down the stairs before he knew what was going on.

I heard him say, "What the hell?"

And then I was out the door and running for the waiting cab.

I didn't get what I came for, but I got something else.

Marta was scared. The Senator had everyone, including the cops, under his thumb. He was even more corrupt and more powerful than I'd imagined.

And that meant his buddy, Katiana, was, as well.

I was going to prove it.

And prove that he'd killed that woman.

10

When I got back to the hotel I found out that Dante and Wayne were somewhere with that duplicitous cow, Katiana.

Dante acted hinky about where they were. I suspected they were at the bank transferring copious amounts of money to that con woman who was making a kid materialize out of thin air.

Anthony wasn't answering the texts I'd sent.

I went up to my room and read and showered and ordered room service as night fell and nobody texted to tell me they were back at the hotel.

I was lonely.

I decided to head to the hotel bar on the first floor.

The dimly lit space was already filled with a few business men hunched over laptops, tablets and phones. One table held an old drunk with a big red nose and a group of women stood at the other end of the bar.

I pulled up a seat at the opposite end. The bartender was cute. He had long wavy hair, a goatee and his muscled arms rippled with thick veins. Three women at the end of the bar were flirting with him, telling him they'd tip him really well if he served their drinks with his shirt off.

It was too bad that he also sported a wedding ring.

Married men were off limits. Even though I loved casual sex and thought nothing of it except the pleasure it gave two people, I had standards. I sure as fuck wasn't a home wrecker.

A guy in a suit and diamond cufflinks sat beside me and ordered me another of "whatever she's drinking."

I pointedly eyed his wedding ring. "Does your wife mind you buying strange women drinks when you're out of town on business?"

"What my wife doesn't know won't hurt her," he said and winked at me.

I glared at him and waved off the bartender who had started to pour me a second drink.

Big mouth kept talking even though I'd turned my entire body away.

"Hey, we're not really married anyway. I mean, we live together and all that, but we really don't have sex anymore. We live separate lives."

"Of course you do." I said.

"We're only together for the kids. As soon as my oldest graduates, we're splitting up. It's sort of an open marriage."

Just then his phone, which was resting on the bar beside us, lit up with a message. We both eyed it.

"Goodnight. Love you. Good luck with your meeting tomorrow. We miss you."

"You're a piece of shit," I said.

He shrugged and smirked standing. "It was worth a shot."

I rolled my eyes. The bartender, who had been busily drying glasses nearby, came over to me.

"You expected to meet someone different at a hotel bar?" he asked.

"I really don't want to meet anyone." I eyed his ring. "You must get hit on all the time."

He nodded. "Yeah. But my wife has nothing to worry about. I'm not interested in anyone else."

I smiled. "In that case, I'm happy to meet you." I lifted my glass to him.

He poured a shot of some amber liquid, clinking his glass to mine.

The bar got busy then and I nursed another two drinks after receiving texts from Dante that he and Wayne were going to bed early and one from Anthony that he'd been roped into a dinner with the Senator and his wife and now they were showing him photos of their recent trip to Cambodia.

The women at the end of the bar stood. One stretched languidly, her already tiny top lifting even higher, her eyes like lasers on the bartender. They stopped behind me on their way out.

"Nathan," one of them said, stretching her arm out beside me pushing a black business card. "If you change your mind about the after party, text me. This is our last night in the city and I want to make it memorable."

He gave her a brilliant smile. "Be safe out there."

Holding the card, he waited until the door closed behind them and then flicked it into the trash.

"Your wife's a lucky woman."

"I'm the lucky one," he said.

Then he placed his palms down on the bar in front of me. "What I don't get is why you're here alone. You seem like good people."

I laughed out loud. "Hardly."

"No, really. What gives? You shouldn't be here alone."

It was a good question.

What could I say? I'd been ditched by my friends and future lover?

"I couldn't sleep."

Just saying that made me yawn.

"But I think I'm good now," I said. "You really helped."

He let out a loud laugh.

"If there's one thing I'm good at, it's boring the women to sleep, that's for sure."

I grinned. "I was a little restless and talking to you and having a drink helped."

I stayed until the bar closed at four in the morning.

The bartender, Nathan, and I talked about the current political climate. Not my favorite topic of conversation but hey, when you're in Rome.

"It's Wednesday so it's slow tonight," he said. "But if you're still here tomorrow, all the big players in D.C. have some super-secret meeting here."

"Really?"

"Yeah. See that door?" He pointed to a door off the side. "That's a backroom. That's where the real deals are made—the ones that nobody talks about."

I nodded.

I put a fifty-dollar bill down. "I'll be back."

He eyed the money. "Don't you think that's excessive."

I rolled my eyes. "Whatever."

I walked out despite his protests about the tip.

In my room, I crawled into bed and fell into a deep sleep.

The next morning, I woke and stretched and was surprised to find I'd slept in until nine. There were texts from Anthony and Dante that I decided to ignore. I was irritated that they'd both blown me off the night before.

Besides I wanted to hit the gym.

The past few months I'd gotten into the habit of getting up early and doing Budo in my hotel suite or at Kato's studio, depending. I followed the martial arts with an hour of meditation before starting my day. It kept my brain from going in directions I didn't want it to go.

I was a killer. But that didn't mean I wanted to think about the people I killed.

I kept their faces in a locked box in my mind.

If I didn't work out or meditate, I'd see them pop up throughout my day, straining at the bars on the locked box, their death faces leering at me, begging me to let them out.

The hotel had a gym so I dressed in black leggings and a black cropped tank top and headed down. The gym was packed but I managed to squeeze into a space in front of the mirror and practice some of my Budo moves. Then I did a series of pushups, pull ups and sit ups until sweat poured down my face.

I was becoming more like my Aunt Eva every day. She was a Sicilian assassin who ran a boot camp training women assassins. She was in amazing physical shape, an expert marksman and trained in the art of Italian sword fighting, gladiatura moderna. She could take down a platoon of men in the blink of an eye.

Unlike me, she didn't drink alcohol to excess, smoke cigarettes or weed or sleep around.

She was a carefully crafted killing machine.

I missed her. And Rose.

When I got back to my room I pulled up their numbers to send a group text.

But when it came time to write a message I didn't know what to say.

"Miss you both."

It was enough.

They both immediately responded.

"Love you, Gia," Rose wrote.

"Come visit," Eva wrote.

I hearted both messages and put my phone down to get in the shower.

My heart ached so bad. Rose was like my very own daughter. But when her father, Nico, had died, she'd taken off and never came back.

I knew she was avoiding me because it hurt too much to see me.

I loved her anyway, but I would give anything to hug her again and try to help with her pain. She was the closest thing I'd ever have to a daughter. She was so precious to me.

As I thought about her, I realized I had tears streaming down my face. God damn it.

I was naked and about to step into the hot water when there was a knock on my door. I grabbed a towel and peered through the peephole. A woman with a bouquet of roses.

White ones.

Not my style.

But I flung the door open.

"Thank you."

They were from Anthony. I handed the woman a twenty dollar bill and plopped the flowers on the counter. There was a thick white card with tiny writing on it. I picked it up and squinted to read the small print. I had to flip the card over to read the note, which was scrawled on both sides. Suddenly I wished I'd tipped that maid more. Especially if she'd been the one who had to fit Anthony's prose on this tiny white card.

"Please accept my apologies. This trip has taken a turn for the worst and apparently, I'm the Senator's whipping boy today, as well. I promise to take you to a wonderful dinner tonight if you'll allow me - Anthony.

"Whatever."

I dialed Dante.

"*Ciao.*"

"Where are you guys?"

"We're touring the National Gallery of Art and then we're meeting with Katiana for lunch."

"Oh, yeah, Katiana—you're new best friend."

"Gia." His voice held a warning tone I ignored.

"Where are you meeting?"

He paused.

"What? I'm not invited."

"Sure, you should join us," he said, covering his tracks. "That's a great idea. I know once you get to know her better you won't be so ..."

He trailed off.

"So what?" I said, frowning.

"So suspicious of her motives."

"I listen to my gut, *paesano*," I said. "I think she's sketchy. So, sue me."

"See you soon," he said and hung up.

I glared at my phone.

I dialed Danny and miracle of miracles he picked up.

"I need every bit of dirt on this bitch you can find."

11

Danny came through.

As always.

He found an article on a blog that mentioned Blondie.

It said that a teenage girl had accused her of kidnapping her and making her into a sex worker.

"Holy shit, D!" I texted back.

"Ikr?!" It was Millennial speak for "I know, right?"

I learned something new all the time from this kid.

"Anything else?"

"I'm still digging," he wrote back. "Gonna find who she was before she was Katiana. Nothing comes up before five years ago. It's as if she didn't exist."

"Really? Very interesting."

I sat down on my couch and read the blog post in depth.

It was called, "That Time I was Sex Trafficked."

Editor's Note: Identifying details and names have either been omitted or changed to protect the author.

My name is Molly. At least for the purposes of this article.

I grew up in a wealthy family in a wealthy neighborhood in Virginia. My parents doted on me and my sister and gave us everything we ever dreamed of, but mostly they gave us their time, love and attention.

But my life is shit now.

It's not their fault.

It's the fault of an evil woman who ruined my life.

I've been in therapy for the past six months but I still wake up every day crying.

A year ago, I was kidnapped by this woman - someone I trusted because she knew my parents. She handed me over to men who flew me in a private jet to Dubai. Besides the kidnapping/against my will part, it doesn't sound too bad, right?

Let me backup, I was yanked out of the college I was attending when I was a junior and excited to start my senior year. I was engaged to an amazing man who adored me and we were planning our wedding right after my college graduation. I'd just got a new puppy and she was the light of my life.

And then, a woman who was a friend of the family, invited me to a special, private party.

She told me that I would meet powerful men there who could make my career. That I could graduate and already have a job with one of the most successful global investment companies in the world. After all I trusted her because my parents did.

But then the thing she said which should have been a red flag was that I shouldn't tell my parents.

"They really want you to do all this on your own and while I respect that, I think it's a little old fashioned. In this town, it's all about who you know," she'd told me.

I agreed. You could be the smartest kid in your graduating class with the highest GPA and all the volunteer work on the planet but if your classmate had a connection he or she would get the job.

My parents hated nepotism and anything that smacked of someone getting a break because of who they know.

My only excuse for lying to them and getting myself in this situation was that I was afraid.

I was so afraid of disappointing them by not getting the job they—and I—had dreamed of.

So I agreed to go to the party.

When I arrived, everyone had on masks. I was escorted to a back room to meet with the CEO of the global financial company. A maid brought me a glass of Champagne while I waited.

I was so nervous that I gulped it down.

The next thing I know I woke up on a private jet. I was in a bedroom on the jet and dressed in lingerie. I panicked but I couldn't walk right or move my body right. I'd obviously been drugged.

Then a series of men came into the bedroom and raped me one after the other until I prayed to God to die.

By the time the jet landed, I had no fight left in me.

I'd been a virgin. I'd been saving myself for my wedding night.

In a few hours, my entire world had been destroyed.

I was taken to a high-rise penthouse in Dubai and kept locked in an apartment that was fit for a king but to me it felt like I'd taken an elevator to the antechamber of hell.

I was repeatedly raped by different men every day. I was starving and thirsty every day so I ate and drank the meager food they gave me even though I knew it was keeping me drugged.

One day I had the willpower to flush the drinks and food down the toilet and started to feel like my old self. That was the day I almost escaped. I managed to punch the next man who tried to lay on top of me. He beat me to a pulp.

I woke up in the hospital.

The nurse said I'd been dropped off out front.

I'd nearly died, the nurse told me. It'd been touch and go. My spleen had ruptured. My kidney had a small laceration. My ribs were broken.

I asked if anyone had come to see me. They said no.

I burst into tears. I was barely this side of death and I was crying tears of happiness.

I was free.

I called my parents. They'd thought I'd run away.

When I told them that our family friend had arranged my kidnapping, they said she'd been distraught and had headed up search efforts.

She told them she had brought me to a party to introduce me to someone for a job and that the staff had seen me drunk and leaving with a sheik she didn't know.

Lies!

But my parents still don't believe me. They still stick up for her, saying I'm delusional to think she was behind it and that she gave thousands of dollars to search for me.

Because they don't believe me I'm now estranged from my family and trying to start a new life for myself.

But I've done some research. This woman has done this to many other young women. Most who never escape.

She also trafficked younger women than me.

She sells children in grade school to sexual predators.

I saw one of them.

While I was being held hostage, a man once brought a girl, a grade-school girl into my room. But the sheik stormed in and grabbed her before anything happened.

I will never forgive myself for not trying to kill him right then.

I was too drugged and weak.

This woman is a monster. The devil incarnate.

This woman, who was a longtime friend of our family, is still friends with my parents. I've come to find out that she is very powerful. If I name her, I'm afraid I'll end up dead.

I threatened to expose her once in a text when I first got back and she said if I do, my little sister is next.

All I can say is that she moves in the most powerful and highest circles of Washington, D.C.

She has white blonde hair.

She's beautiful. And deadly.

And by the way, her initials are K.D.

When I first got back to the states, she was arrested, but then, miraculously the cop who believed me and arrested her was fired and then she was set free without any charges ever being filed. Like I said, she's very very powerful.

I PRINTED OUT THE ARTICLE.

It wasn't the proof I'd hoped for, but it was close enough. It had to be her.

The party. The sex trafficking. The selling of young girls. Powerful in Washington, D.C. circles. Blonde. Beautiful. Connected.

I texted Anthony.

"What's Katiana's last name?"

He responded Demonde.

Boom. K.D. I wanted to puke.

Armed with the printed-out article, I decided to head to lunch and see what Blondie had to say about it.

I walked into the restaurant and plunked three copies of the blog post down - one copy for each of them. I saw Blondie's eyes flicker down to it and then back up. She smiled at me and it was an evil fucking smile.

Fear trickled through me.

I sat down.

"I see you found the article my poor goddaughter wrote in the middle of her breakdown."

"Her breakdown?"

Dante looked up. He held up the papers.

"What is this?"

"An article about Katiana. Right, Katiana?"

She gave me a tight smile.

"Tori is my goddaughter. She's mentally unstable. She has a long history of mental illness. You can look it up. Her name is Margaret Carlton. She went off the deep end about a year ago. She is delusional and a drug addict. They found her in a crack house outside of the district here mumbling about being raped by sheiks in Dubai. It is all very, very sad.

"What about the arrest she mentioned?"

There had to be records of that, right?

"There was an arrest," Katiana said silkily. "But it was the woman who gave her drugs at the party I took her too. You can look that up too. Her name is Lorna Radikovich. She drugged Tori at the party and got her hooked-on drugs which is how Tori ended up in that crack house for six months."

"I don't think so," I said. "I think she's telling the truth."

I met her eyes. She seemed calm but her eyes sent daggers at me.

"Gia," Dante said in a low, dangerous voice. "Please leave. You Are embarrassing us and yourself."

I felt the color drain from my face. He believed her, not me.

"What?" I said, not quite believing it. I'd honestly thought he would back me. He'd drank the Kool-Aid. He was so eager to adopt that he refused to see what was right in front of him.

"Gia, I'm concerned."

I clamped my lips together and stood. I paused for a second, but realized there was nothing I could say. I would have to prove it. Outside on my walk back to the hotel, I wanted to cry. It hurt so bad that Dante believed that witch over me.

By the time I got back to the hotel, I was slightly calmer.

Once there, I pulled out my laptop to find out what I could about this Radikovich woman.

I found an article about her arrest. It said she was involved in sex trafficking.

About a year before the arrest, she'd opened a small public relations firm. It didn't seem to fit.

I then searched court records. She was sentenced to 16 months in jail.

I searched jail records. She was not an inmate anywhere I could find.

I searched arrest records. Nothing.

I texted Danny saying I couldn't find any records on her arrest or conviction or jail time through the regular channels and hoped he could.

I then did a more in-depth search for any other articles on her.

That's when I found a small obituary for her. I clicked on the legacy page. There were only a few memories. A few said they hoped she'd rot in hell.

One, however, said that they believed she was framed and that they refused to believe she killed herself in jail.

Holy shit.

That post was anonymous.

I sat back and thought about it. Maybe the journalist who wrote the article about her arrest knew something.

I dialed the number at the bottom of the article. His name was Kendall Kendicott.

"Newsroom. Kendicott."

"Hi, I'm wondering if you could tell me about Lorna Radikovich. I saw you wrote an article about her."

The line was silent.

"Hello?"

"Who is this?" he was whispering, sort of hissing.

"An old friend of hers."

"I can't help you."

"Wait! Don't hang up. I can't find the arrest reports about her or any sign that she served time in jail and yet they said she committed suicide in jail. What's up with that?"

"You're making a mistake even calling me. If you know what's good for you, you'll quit asking questions. Don't ever call me again."

Then he hung up.

What the fuck.

I dialed again. It went straight to voicemail

A text appeared from Danny.

"She's a ghost. Only thing I could find was the obituary and an article by some punk ass with a stupid name.

"Kendall Kendicott."

"Yeh."

I told Danny about Kendicott blowing me off.

"Dude."

"Ikr," I typed.

12

I tossed my phone on the bed, picked up the room phone, and ordered two fat Martinis from room service.

While I waited for room service I emptied my mini bar, downing anything that had alcohol in it.

I was going to drown my sorrows in booze. At least for a few hours.

I was so frustrated. I was worried that without being able to prove it, I'd made things worse.

Now, Dante would never believe me.

Not only that, he hated my guts.

That deep-seated rage he probably felt about Matt's death had been unleashed.

I wanted to cry. But I held it back.

But my only option was to prove him wrong.

To show him I wasn't acting crazy because of the adoption trauma I had.

I needed to prove that Katiana was a crook.

I fell asleep sprawled diagonally on my bed.

I woke with a raging headache and dry mouth and makeup smeared around my eyes.

I checked my phone to see if Dante had apologized.

Nothing. But Anthony had texted and asked me to meet him in the lobby at eight. I gave his text a thumbs up and looked at the time.

Six-thirty.

I showered and dressed quickly and headed to the hotel bar.

I wasn't sure where we were going for dinner, but as a subtle act of rebellion I ignored the silky navy wrap dress with Dante's note that said, "For dinners in Washington."

Instead, I pulled on my favorite soft as butter leather dress that had a modest neckline and fell to my knees but obscenely hugged every curve. I paired it with my favorite Fuck Me stilettos with the silver studs.

Nathan gave a low whistle when I walked in.

"Hey, good looking," he said.

"Patrón, please, my friend," I said. "What time do all the VIP's get here usually?"

"Late. Midnight."

"What about Senator Mitchell? Is he part of the Rat Pack?"

"Like clockwork. Every Thursday. He runs the show."

I wondered if Anthony was going to be invited this week since he was in town.

"If I come down before midnight, how can I get into that room?"

He scrunched up his face thinking. "Good question. Let me think about it. Why? You CIA?"

"I wish."

"But you have a dog in this hunt?"

"I might."

He nodded.

"Got a question for you," I said, taking a sip of my tequila. "Is it pretty common practice for any crime or wrongdoing to be covered up by the cops in this city?"

He lowered his voice. "The bigger the crime, the bigger the cover up."

"So a murder at a party with all the city's movers and shakers wouldn't make the news?"

"Not unless Lois Lane herself was at the party and witnessed it."

I frowned. "That's bullshit. I hate that."

"Me, too, sister," he said. "Me, too."

"What if I pretended to be Lois Lane?"

"You don't want to be Lois Lane. Trust me. You won't like what happens to Lois Lane. Superman does not come save her. At least not in Washington, D.C."

"Oh yeah?" I said. "What happens to people like Lois Lane?"

"They disappear."

"Huh?" I said. "All you have to do is get me in that room at midnight."

"I'll do my best."

I slid a piece of paper with my number on it.

"Text me if you come up with a plan."

"Deal."

I finished my drink and headed to the lobby to meet Anthony.

When I first saw him, I searched his face to see if Dante had squealed about my less than impressive performance at lunch.

But he had a big grin and kissed me smack on the lips.

I liked it.

Once we'd climbed in the limo he put his hand on my thigh and I scooted closer in the dark.

Anthony briefed me in the limo that if he received the backing of the old stodgy representative we were dining with, a lot of the dude's cronies would fall in line.

"Once I'm in power, I can ignore all their racists, sexist, bullshit," he said. "But for now, I'm walking the line."

"Sounds awful," I said.

"Oh trust me. It is." Anthony said. "That's why I end up drinking way too much on these trips. It's also why I practically begged you to come with me. I knew you would keep me focused and centered."

"Really?" I said. "Is it working?"

He sighed. "It is. When I see you, I remember my values and why I'm running for senate in the first place."

I was surprised.

All too soon, we pulled in front of the restaurant. He held my hand to help me out of the car. Inside, we were seated at a large table where I met some stuffy politicians that he was trying to impress so they would support him in his campaign.

At least that was my read on it.

I was bored to tears. But I smiled and played along.

Sitting with the old farts through a three-hour dinner was excruciating.

I bit my tongue about one billion times.

It was clear that their stance on issues was purely for political reasons. What they thought privately was disturbing at best and disgusting at the worst.

They only gave a fuck about themselves, amassing wealth and getting re-elected.

Anthony had the balls to argue with them, but only when they said the most egregiously sexist and racist things. They just laughed.

Once during dinner. I leaned over and asked Anthony why he wasn't hanging out with Senator Mitchell that night.

He'd shrugged. "Not sure. He has some standing meeting every Thursday night that I'm apparently not invited to."

I was relieved to hear that. It meant Anthony wasn't in on whatever the boys in the back room were doing. I already suspected it was fucked up.

I leaned over and spontaneously kissed his cheek.

He gave me a wry grin. "Does this mean we are having a sleepover tonight?" he whispered, reaching under the table to caress my leg.

I didn't answer.

I couldn't wait to leave. But not the reason Anthony probably hoped for.

I kept glancing at my watch. I needed to be back to the hotel before midnight. Nathan had texted me. He had a plan to get me in the back room.

Finally, the dinner was over. Anthony kissed me in the car and I practically crawled into his lap. It was no surprise that he rode up in the elevator and walked me to the door of my hotel room.

Damn. He was hot. He pressed me up against the door and kissed me.

I wriggled out from under him. It was 11:30 p.m. I had to be downstairs in minutes. Or less.

"I'm sorry, I don't think it's going to happen tonight," I said.

"No nightcap, then?"

"Not tonight, Romeo."

"Aye, aye, Captain."

He smiled and nodded. Then he saluted me and I realized he had drank more than I'd initially realized.

"Probably good. I drank too much to take the edge off and not argue with those old fucks and now I think I need to go sleep it off."

For a split-second I wondered if he was lying. Was he pretending and then heading down to the hotel bar and the back room gathering? I'd soon find out.

"Sleep well, Anthony." I leaned over and kissed his cheek and then smiled as I closed the door.

With my ear pressed against the door, I listened to his footsteps approach the elevators and then the ding as the doors opened.

I waited a beat and then quickly scrubbed every ounce of makeup off my face. I patted some stage makeup on to hide my scar. Even though it had been hidden under my large eye mask at the party, I still didn't want anything that would easily identify me to any of these men. Usually I didn't hide the scar at all. It was part of me.

I absentmindedly fingered my scar. It ran from my cheekbone up to my hairline. It was a reminder of King, an evil fucker who managed to cut my face and murder at least ten people, including my friend Ethel, in his sick ethnic cleansing operation. He'd made the FBI Most Wanted list before I found him and took him out.

The theater makeup I had worked its job.

I yanked my hair back in a tight ponytail and grabbed some oversized fake eyeglasses. Then I quickly changed into black jeans and a white dress shirt that used to belong to Nico and that I sometimes slept in.

I gave myself one last glance in the mirror and stepped outside. It was time to see just what the big boys had planned and if I recognized any of them from the night before.

I hoped that with the help of the mask I'd worn the other night and the disguise, I wouldn't be recognized.

When I got to the bar, I strapped on the black apron Nathan had waiting for me.

"You look different," he said.

"Good," I said and stuck out my hand. "KellyAnn, at your service."

13

I GOT TO THE BAR AT 12:10 A.M.

Nathan said the men were always punctual and would be in the room waiting for a waitress at that time.

A short, tattooed waitress with a black bob gave me a dirty look while Nathan filled my tray with another round of drinks for the back room.

He'd told her that I'd be working her regular gig by "special request."

By the sneer on her face, I could tell she didn't like it. Or me. At all.

I felt sort of bad for her so I was planning on giving her any tips I made that night to make up for honing in on her business.

I didn't want the money.

I wanted the access.

I loaded up my tray with the men's "regular" orders that Nathan had prepared.

When I first walked into the back room, checking the door with my hip since my hands were full, a ripple of alarm seemed to race through the room.

One guy immediately pushed back his chair and stood.

"Who are you? Where's Sara?"

"I'm KellyAnn," I said, giving him a bright smile. I hoped my fake Southern accent would dispel any familiarity about me because I recognized the guy from the party. His gray-streaked black hair swept back in a familiar way. And then of course there was the senator, sitting at the far end of the table bossing everyone around.

For a split second when I'd walked in and he'd looked up, fear spiked through me but his gaze glanced off my face and immediately went to my chest, which, thank God, was adequately covered up by Nico's white blouse.

"Sorry, fellas," I said. "I'm new today so y'all are gonna have to tell me which drink is yours."

The guy who had first questioned me remained standing. The man beside him put his hand on his sleeve as if to stop him from whatever he was about to do.

"Where's our regular server?" he said.

"Like I said, sugar pie, I'm new. I told the bartender I didn't want to serve the louts out in the main room."

I paused.

"My experience is with, let's just say, more refined, gentlemen," I said and winked.

That seemed to settle them down. The guy sat back down in his seat and smiled. "Come here for a second and I'll help you figure out which drink goes where," he said.

I walked over and before I knew it, he'd wrapped his arm around my waist, placing his palm on my ass. For a second I imagined my elbow smashing his nose into smithereens and my sharp nails poking into his eyeballs.

But I did none of that. Instead I squirmed away, keeping the smile plastered on my face.

"You men just let me know which drink is yours. I'm a fast learner. I'll have it memorized by next time."

Soon, I'd dispersed most of the drinks on my side of the room.

I felt the senator's eyes on me at the far end of the table.

Any semblance of being a gentleman had disappeared from him.

That facade he had at the party was gone. his true predatory and piggish nature was on full display in this back room.

He crooked a finger at me. Fuck. Did he recognize me?

I walked over. "Which one is yours?" I said with a big smile.

"That one," he said.

I put it in front of him and turned to move away when he spoke.

"I was wondering if I could order something special from you tonight?"

He spoke in such a low voice I had to lean over to hear him. Too late I realized it had given him the perfect opportunity to look down my blouse. I decided to fasten the top buttons as soon as I left the room.

As if he was reading my mind, the senator said, "We old guys don't touch but we do like to look so if you really want to make us happy you might want to undo a button or two on your blouse. Because when we are happy we tip really, really well if you know what I mean."

He took a one-hundred-dollar bill and slid it under his glass.

I gave him a smile. "I always make my customers happy, sir," I said and then added," When you say you old guys don't touch do you mean your colleague over there who grabbed my back end when I first got here."

He frowned.

"Nicholson!" he bellowed. "Why don't you apologize to the lady for disrespecting her."

The entire room grew quiet.

The man cleared his throat. "My apologies."

"Accepted," I said and gave a slight bow."

Then I slipped away and back into the main bar area.

"How'd it go?" Nathan asked in a low voice.

"Nearly unbearable, but that's what I expected," I said.

I didn't tell him it would take all my willpower to bite my tongue and keep from punching a few of the men. Instead I would grit my teeth and play the game.

"Yeah. They're a bunch of douchebags," he said.

"Totally," I said and made eye contact with the sulky brunette. She made a face. I wondered how she could put up with their shit every week. I suddenly felt bad for her.

"How can I stay there longer than just dropping off drinks?" I asked Nathan when the other server moved away.

"Let me think about that," he said.

He moved to the other side of the bar and served a few drinks. Then he came back.

"I don't know," he said. "Well, I do know, but I don't think that's what you had in mind."

"Nope. Not what I had in mind."

He laughed.

"I just want to be the fly on the wall. I'd like to be able to hear what they are talking about."

"They have a guy come in and sweep the room for bugs before anyone else arrives. They are obviously talking about some top-secret shit."

"Yeah," I said. "They shut up as soon as I walked in and they were pretty suspicious of me at first. I wouldn't even know how to bug a room anyway."

That got me thinking.

But I knew how to hit the record button on my phone. I needed a place to hide it and a way to get it in.

Just then a tray was carried in from the kitchen. It contained food for the back room - another standing order. There were two large bread baskets. They each contained a thick napkin that had bread piled on top. Carefully I lifted the napkin with the bread slices out of one of the baskets. I put my phone down inside the basket and hit record. I lifted the thick napkin with the bread loaded on it and put it on top of my phone.

I had no idea if it would work, but it was worth a shot.

A bus boy helped me carry the large tray inside the room. I put the bread basket near Senator Mitchell's end of the table.

The bus boy placed the other one at the other side of the table.

We passed out the appetizers they had ordered and then slipped out of the room.

I waited impatiently for time to pass where I could reasonably go back in and ask to refill drinks. I was hoping to keep the bread basket in for the entire time they were there. But that might not work. I was also nervous that someone had found my phone and that they were deciding what to do about it. I worried I hadn't put the phone on silent, but I knew I had. I was just being paranoid.

After a while I went back in. I tried not to look at the bread basket. but out of the corner of my eye I saw it was still there. It hadn't moved. I took orders for drink refills. I was about to leave when the Senator cleared his throat. I turned and he was holding out his plate to me.

"We're done here. Can you please clear our places?"

Fuck.

I gave him a bright smile.

"I'll be right back."

"Oh, one other thing. More bread please."

I turned, alarmed but the basket was still on the table. He

hadn't lifted it up. But were his words loaded? I walked back over and took the bread basket.

"I'll be right back with your drinks and more bread and have Javier come clear your places."

"Thanks sugar."

My heart was pounding when I made it out to the main room. I gave Nathan the drink order, retrieved my phone from the bottom of the empty bread basket and said I'd be right back.

In a bathroom stall, I hit play. The sound quality was crap. I could only make out a few words. I strained to understand what the garbled voices were saying.

Then I heard a few familiar words. Party. Problem. Dead.

Fuck. They had been talking about the party the night before. I knew it. It was the same crowd.

But the recording proved nothing.

I went back to the bar and took off my apron.

"Nathan, I'm not feeling well," I said and glanced at the tattooed brunette. "Can someone else finish up the back room?"

"Georgia?"

"I'll do it," the brunette said, rolling her eyes.

"You can have the tips. I just got sick in the bathroom. I think the oysters I had at lunch were bad," I said, making a face. "Food poisoning."

I clutched my stomach and rushed out.

I hoped that my sudden disappearance didn't arouse suspicion and that she would convey the message that I was food poisoned.

The last thing I wanted to do was get her or Nathan in trouble.

I'd wasted my time. All I'd done was find out where D.C.'s major players were every Thursday night.

I stepped inside the elevator and hit my floor right when I

saw a familiar blonde head step into a cab on the sidewalk outside the lobby.

I would've swore it was Katiana.

I tried to hit "open" on the elevator door but by the time it did and I rushed out onto the sidewalk there was no sign of her or the cab.

14

THE NEXT MORNING WE ALL FLEW BACK TO SAN FRANCISCO IN THE private jet that Anthony apparently had at his beck and call.

I was disappointed.

My few days in Washington D.C. going to fancy parties and having sex with Anthony had turned into a bust.

Nothing had happened as I'd expected.

Instead, I was frantic to prove that Dante and Wayne were getting mixed up in some deep dark shit by adopting a child from that blonde witch.

Dante and Wayne had both pointedly ignored me on the ride to the airport.

At one point Wayne had given me a sympathetic pout before Dante glared at him.

Once we boarded the plane, they made a point to sit in the back seats far away from where Anthony had settled us into the front of the plane.

When I got up to use the restroom, I saw reams of paper spread on the small table before them. They were filling out the paperwork to adopt the girl in the picture they'd shown me.

"Hey," I said after I used the bathroom, pausing at their seats. "Did Katiana come to the hotel to see you guys last night?"

Dante's tone was icy. "No. Why? Did you want to embarrass yourself even more?"

Fuck you.

But I didn't say anything.

When I returned to my seat I saw immediately that Anthony had heard. He raised an eyebrow.

"Are you and Dante on the outs?"

I shrugged. "Something like that."

"I hope it was nothing I did being so busy and caught up in all that political nonsense."

I laughed. "Isn't political nonsense your life's calling?"

He smirked.

"What do you know about Katiana?" I asked him.

Dante made a noise from the back of the plane that I ignored.

"Not much except that it seems that every one who is anyone in Washington knows her and seems to like her."

"I don't."

Anthony burst into laughter. "She's a bit of a prickly pear toward women."

I lowered my voice. It was time to test the waters with Anthony and see just how much he trusted his godfather.

"I think she had something to do with that woman's death and I think her adoption business is a scam. Did you say it was the senator who recommended her?"

Before he could answer, Dante was out of his seat.

"Give it up, Gia," Dante said from the back of the plane. "It's none of your business."

"I don't trust her," I said.

"You don't have to," said Dante who had walked to our seats to butt into my conversation with Anthony.

"I do have to trust her," I said. "If my best friend is paying her a hundred thousand dollars to adopt a child in a fucking hinky way I have to know I trust her."

"My money. My life, Gia."

Anthony let out a slow whistle. "That's what she charges? No wonder she can afford the lifestyle she has."

Dante was bristling.

"I don't know what your problem is, Gia," he said. "I'd think you would be happy that we're going to be parents."

"I'm very happy about your decision to adopt and I think any kid who has you and Wayne for parents will be the luckiest child in the world," I said calmly, "but I don't trust that woman for as far as I can throw her."

"Okay. You've spoken your piece, now let it go. You've already embarrassed us enough."

'Better embarrassed than fucking broke from some con artist."

Dante huffed away.

I flagged down the attendant and ordered two doubles.

Once I downed them both in a row, Anthony spoke up.

"Gia," he said in a low voice. "I'm sorry about that. And I'm sorry that this trip didn't turn out the way I'd wanted. I'd really hoped to spend time with you. It seems if you are a senatorial candidate, you have to do what everyone else says. I don't like it. But I have to play the game."

"Uh huh."

"And to make matters worse, I have to go over all this paperwork for the city. There's just not enough time in the day."

"Yup."

Again, my response was dry.

He shifted in his seat.

"You didn't answer my question," I said.

"I have to trust the people my godfather recommends. I've known him my whole life."

"We're going to have to disagree then. This might be a deal-breaker for me. I think he's…"

I cut off my words. I wanted to say he was a stone-cold killer.

"He wouldn't hurt a fly," Anthony said. "He's harmless. A bit arrogant but harmless."

"What if I told you I thought he killed that woman at the party?"

"What?"

Dante was back up by our seats.

"Gia have you told Anthony about … you know … your breakdown?"

I glared at him, speechless.

He turned to Anthony. "We think that our adoption has triggered something that was very traumatic for Gia. I'll let her tell you herself. She thinks she saw something at the party but she's hallucinated before under stress. She was very inebriated."

I looked at Dante in astonishment.

He was crying. Seeing tears drip down his face only made me angrier.

"Gia," he said. "the only reason I'm saying something is because I love you and I'm concerned. Very concerned."

"Dante," I said with a voice of steel. "Fuck. You."

Before he could answer, I stood and rushed to the bathroom. I stood with my hands on the sink looking at my face in the mirror. My cheeks were flushed from the alcohol and pure, unadulterated rage. I was mortified and beginning to question everything. Dante was gas lighting me. The one person I thought I could count on in every situation.

After a few minutes, I came out of the bathroom and strapped back in next to Anthony. I didn't know what the fuck to say.

"I'm so sorry," he said.

"About what?" I said in a cold voice. "I know what I saw and heard."

He shook his head and didn't answer. I put on my sunglasses and air pods and cranked the Beastie Boys until our descent into San Francisco.

Anthony's car dropped us off at our hotel.

He walked me to the elevator.

"I wish I could stay," he said.

I didn't answer, just stared at his mouth and pulled his shirt so his body was pressed up against mine.

"Gia," he began.

"Goodnight," I said and stepped into the elevator.

I got a text on the way to my floor.

"You drive me wild."

"Prove it."

"I will. Soon."

But I didn't see him again for another week.

He texted me every day. He never said a word about my conversation with Dante on the plane. I sent him seductive, but not revealing, pictures of me. My torso with a towel covering everything but my clavicle. A shot of my legs in high heels kicked up on the balcony rail. A close up of my lips painted red and pouted.

"You are driving me mad," he'd write.

"Apparently not enough or you'd be here right now," I wrote back one night.

"On my way."

"Door is unlocked."

"I wish." he wrote and sent me a picture of him sitting at his desk in city hall with the windows showing the dark sky behind him. He looked weary with dark circles under his eyes and his hair mussed.

"They don't pay you enough to be working at midnight," I said.

"Tell me about it."

Meanwhile, Dante and I hadn't spoken or texted since our argument on the plane.

It felt like I was missing an arm not texting him every day, but I was furious with him and really hurt by his betrayal. He not only didn't believe me, he made me look bad in front of Anthony.

The only thing to do was to prove Blondie was a crook before the adoption went through.

Even if Dante never forgave me and we never spoke again, I had to stop him from making the biggest mistake of his life.

But it was easier said than done.

I had Danny trying to dig up more dirt on the woman, but he said she seemed to have magically appeared on the Washington scene five years ago and there wasn't a thing about her before that.

"She's fake," I said. "She's made up."

"For sure," Danny said.

At a loss as to how to prove Blondie and Senator Mitchell were stone-cold killers, I kept busy working on the plans for the hotel. We had just started construction on the tenth and eleventh floors. We were remodeling one floor at a time. It meant lost income from the rooms we normally would have booked during this time of year, but it was necessary.

Each day I didn't get shitfaced in my hotel room, I donned a construction hat and oversaw the construction, meeting with the foreman to make sure everything was done according to spec.

There were a surprising number of complications.

Each morning, I scanned the Washington, D.C. newspapers and blogs online. There still was no mention of the dead woman.

But there was news of Senator Mitchell and his campaign. With less than a week left until the election, he was tied in the polls with his opponent.

Then I found a little gossipy tidbit on a blog when I searched up his name.

A woman had accused him of sexual harassment when she'd worked for him.

She'd gone on record with a local radio show host and then when the Washington reporters tried to interview her about it, she retracted her statement.

The reporter said that a close friend of the woman revealed the retraction had been made because the woman was scared for her life.

Of course she was.

15

The next night, I'd just crawled into bed when Anthony texted me.

"Senator Mitchell is in town," he wrote. "We are embarking on a last-minute push, a crazy campaign fundraising trip up and down the coast. I'd love it if you'd come with me."

I remembered that intern had mentioned a trip to California. What was her name? Meg? If I saw her again, I'd warn her about the senator.

"I'm starting to think I'm your beard," I wrote back. "I come along on your trips but really spend no time with you at all."

I could almost hear his laughter in his response even though we were just texting. "Oh, Gia, if only I were gay it would be so much easier. But I'm not going to lie, my desire to have you accompany me is twofold - to spend more time with you, but yes, having a gorgeous successful woman on my arm doesn't hurt with my fundraising efforts."

"I would think it would be a turnoff to all the MILFS with money who are lusting after you."

"It just spurs them to try harder, my darling."

"Huh."

At least he was honest.

I glanced at my calendar. The construction was on hold for a few days next week as they waited for some back-ordered windows.

"I'm free."

"I'll pick you up tomorrow afternoon. Bring all your fancy frocks."

"Have we met?"

"You'll do fine. Bring some heels and a black dress. Even if you wear the same thing every night, you'll still be the most stunning woman in the room."

"Ha."

"If only Dante didn't hate me he could dress me."

"You'd be perfect in a potato sack," he wrote back.

But of course he didn't believe that and reached out to Dante because within twenty minutes, Dante had sent me photos of my outfits for the trip. He had a file with pictures of all my clothes. Which made sense since he'd bought all of them.

"I'm doing this for Anthony not you. I wouldn't want him to lose because his companion is dressed like a homeless woman," he texted.

"Fuck off," I wrote back.

He ignored that and wrote back, "I spoke to Anthony and he sent me your itinerary. Here is what you wear for each day and each event."

I glanced at the photos.

Apparently today when I was picked up, I was supposed to wear a silky red slip type dress with simple strappy black heels and a gold Cleopatra bracelet that snaked up my arm. We were driving straight to Carmel and a party.

Done.

"Put your lipstick in the crossbody Chanel bag," he wrote.

It was a quilted black bag with a gold chain that I'd made

sure fit my phone, lipstick, cigarette case and my smallest gun—my Double Tap .45.

Thank god that even when Dante hated me he wanted me to dress well. I had been planning on wearing some white leather pants and a white strapless top with gold heels. Apparently, that wasn't going to work. It seems I would never learn to dress myself.

Fine by me.

Anthony came to my hotel suite to get me.

I opened the door with a white towel wrapped about me. It barely covered me.

"Am I early?" he asked and genuinely looked confused.

I let the towel drop. "Are you?"

He looked me up and down and then closed his eyes for a second, exhaling loudly.

I waited.

His eyes flicked open.

"Gia? Is this really how you want our first time to be?"

"Anthony, we're not virgins. It's not like our first time needs to be special with red roses and candlelight."

"Maybe it doesn't need to be that way for you," he said and turned. "I'll be waiting in the hall."

I dressed and when I stepped outside my room he smiled at me.

"Maybe this is a bad idea," he said.

"Why?" I said and lit a cigarette.

His eyes flicked to the no smoking sign.

"I own this fucking hotel," I said.

When I opened my bag to put my cigarette case back in it, he saw the gun.

"Must you bring that?"

I eyed him. It did make the bag droopy and heavy.

"The place is going to be thick with security. Nobody is going to get hurt."

"You promise?"

"Yes."

"Why do you think this is a bad idea?" I said.

He shrugged. "It just seems like we keep getting off on the wrong foot."

"Because I think your godfather is a scumbag killer?"

He didn't answer, just hit the down button on the elevator.

We drove straight to the Monterey Peninsula.

Anthony had arranged for us to have wine and snacks in the car.

I nibbled on cheese and crackers and salamis and drank a chilled white wine.

We had finished two bottles by the time we pulled into Monterey.

The conversation had been stilted. I wondered what the fuck I was doing with him anyway.

But then I saw the side of him that made me want to run my fingers through his hair and jump in bed with him.

When we pulled into Monterey, I was struck with dread. I suddenly couldn't get enough air in my lungs. My ears filled with a strange white noise. My heart was thumping so hard I wondered if I was having a heart attack.

Anthony immediately noticed.

"Gia?" he said coming over near me and grabbing my hands. "Are you okay?"

I shook my head.

"What can I do?" he asked. He was so sincere and so concerned and sweet.

"I don't know. I can't breathe."

"Here," he said grabbing both my hands in his. "Hold my hands tight and close your eyes. Now breath with me."

I did as he said and he began to breathe with me counting slowly to ten.

When he was done, I opened my eyes.

He was right before me. The look on his face. He cared for me more than he'd ever let on. I could see it so clearly.

"Any better?" he asked.

I smiled and nodded.

"I had no idea that would happen. I couldn't breathe and my heart was pounding like it was going to leap out of my chest."

"Panic attack," he said. "I occasionally suffer from them. They are hell on earth."

"I don't get it," I said. "I've seen and experienced horrific things, situations that should've fucked me up for life and yet pulling into my hometown makes me have my first panic attack? What the fuck?"

Anthony laughed.

"I think we underestimate the power that our childhoods have on us."

"Fact," I said.

He handed me a glass of water and then smoothed my hair back.

Fuck, why did he have to be so nurturing and sweet?

"There's just so many memories here. Some happy. Some dark," I said.

"Tell me about it."

What to tell him? Did I tell him I'd been raped in Carmel and when I killed my attacker, it had set me on my life course as a killer? Did I tell him I'd fallen in love with Dante in a wooded area over there not knowing he was gay and in love with my psychopathic brother? Did I tell him I'd been called a Dago and Wop by the girls at my middle school over that way and that it had caused my dad to enroll me in my first martial arts class?

I decided instead to tell him a little bit about how growing up here as an Italian had been both a blessing and a curse. I could get hired by any local business person based on my last name alone.

I'd walked into one interview and the owner had said, "Aha, I knew from your last name you were a good Italian girl."

On the other hand, there were also the slurs made by my WASP classmates and the insinuations that my father was a criminal.

"That's rough," Anthony said, reaching for my hand. "Do you think it's still like that here?"

I shrugged. I no longer cared.

"Did Dante experience the same thing?"

I shook my head. "No. He was somehow untouchable. I'm not sure why. Everyone at school just let him be."

The only person who treated him like shit was his dad, I thought but didn't say.

Anthony's phone beeped. He squinted at it and then pulled his hand away sitting up straight.

"I need to make a call," he said.

"Go right ahead," I said.

He hesitated. "To Mitchell."

I shrugged.

He punched in a number and I heard Senator Mitchell's voice answer.

"Are you almost here?"

"About ten minutes out," Anthony said.

We pulled up to the guard house at the entrance to Pebble Beach on 17-Mile-Drive.

Anthony rolled down his window.

The fresh-faced guard in his gray uniform spoke to the

driver and then asked him to roll down the back window. He came over and peered into the back seat at us.

"Welcome, Mayor Ferraro."

The guard's eyes flicked over me, mostly eyeballing my bare legs.

Then he was gone, waving us past.

A few miles down the winding road, past the golf course and some amazing views of the ocean, we stopped at a driveway with a heavy iron gate. The house beyond was not visible, shaded by thick groves of trees.

Another guard, this time dressed in a black uniform and wearing a gun in a visible holster, spoke to the driver for a few moments and then asked Anthony to roll down his window. He came over and stuck his head inside, making eye contact with me for a long moment and then asked us for identification. I bristled but dug into my bag for my I.D. and handed it to Anthony.

The guard took the I.D.'s back to the guard house and that's when I saw them.

Three guys in dark suits with ear pieces and dark sunglasses even though dusk had fallen.

Secret Service.

After a few minutes, the guard came back and handed back our I.D.'s without a word.

He turned and walked away. The gates swung open and our driver stepped on the gas. A little too much. I was jolted back into my seat.

The house was about a half mile up from the road.

It was a white Tudor-style home with all its windows lit up like a homing beacon.

A team of valets waited to rush over and open our doors. Our driver seemed annoyed.

A man in a tuxedo escorted us through the house to a

magical backyard. It was like an enchanted forest, strung with fairy lights and lanterns. Groups of people milled about and low music played. The turquoise light from a series of connecting pools lit people's faces with a soft glow. Tiki torches were scattered around the thick trees surrounding the main patio area.

A woman in green silk looked over as we entered and made her way toward us, leaving the group she was speaking to.

"Anthony!" the woman said with genuine pleasure as she got closer. She gave him an air kiss and then drew back looking at me expectantly.

"This is Gia Santella," Anthony said.

The woman tilted her head just slightly as if she'd recognized my name.

Then she turned back to Anthony and they talked about his father. Apparently, she was an old friend. I tuned them out and scanned the crowd below us on the patio.

I felt someone's eyes on me.

Motherfucker. It was Senator Mitchell He gave me the once over, his gaze traveling from my head to toe in a creepy manner. A woman was by his side. She noticed his attention and also was staring at me.

I didn't look away. Did he recognize me as the waitress from the back room in D.C.? He'd only ever seen me as Gia at the masked party.

Now, my hair was down, I had makeup on, and didn't have the glasses, but his gaze lingered a bit too long.

Fuck me.

What had I gotten myself into?

16

A waitress appeared and blocked my view of the senator. I gratefully scooped a glass of some type of alcohol off the tray and downed it. By the time the waitress moved, I could no longer see the senator. I casually scanned for him in the crowd trying not to make it obvious.

He had disappeared.

Anthony steered us down toward a group that contained Senator Wendy Moore.

Her smile was directed at me when we walked up.

"Gia!" she said. "I'm so glad you came, too."

"Thanks. I'm so happy to support Anthony in any way I can."

She reached for my arm. "I really appreciate it."

I bristled. Why would she appreciate it?

"Do you mind if I borrow Anthony for a moment?" she said.

"Of course not."

She led Anthony away toward a small path that seemed to go deep into the woods. As soon as they left, I made a beeline in the direction where I'd seen Senator Mitchell. Maybe if I got closer I could get a read on whether he knew I was the woman from the hotel bar.

As I made my way through the crowd I saw the intern. Even without the mask, I could recognize her. Her long brown hair, her slim tall build. Her wide smile. Without her mask, I saw she was beautiful. There was something about her—some glow. Then I saw what she was looking at. Senator Mitchell.

Fuck. She was in love with him.

It was obvious.

Then he looked over at her.

Fuck me. They were having an affair.

His wife with her silver blonde hair caught the glance between the two and tightened her hand on the senator's sleeve.

Oh shit. Meg the intern was in over her head. His wife knew for sure.

Then his eyes met mine. Double fuck.

A Secret Service guy came up and said something to the senator, who, in response, leaned over and said something to his wife and then headed toward the house.

Then the wife did something interesting, she walked straight over to Meg. I was close enough to hear the conversation.

"I'd like it if you would prepare our itinerary for tomorrow and have it waiting when we wake in the morning at five?"

I saw Meg flush from her neck up.

"Of course."

"You might want to go get started on it now," the wife said. "I'll have them call you a car."

I wanted to stay and defend Meg, but I wanted to see where Senator Mitchell had gotten off to. I wanted to see if he recognized me. I needed to know if I was in any danger. Or, more importantly, if Anthony was in danger because of my actions.

I already knew that people ended up dead because of this man.

I knew it deep down inside, even if I couldn't prove it.

I was torn because I also wanted to get Meg alone and warn

her that the senator might not be who she thought he was. If she was having an affair with him and he was a criminal, she could be complicit without even knowing anything.

Just then my phone dinged. A text from Danny with a link. I had no idea what it was but I clicked on the link.

Motherfuck. The journalist I'd called was dead. He'd been mugged and beaten to death walking home from the paper to his apartment the night before.

I exhaled. I knew why he was dead.

They knew I'd called him about Blondie.

Inside the house, I looked for the senator and when I didn't see him, I headed toward a large staircase.

At the top was a hall that led in two directions.

I heard voices from the right so I started that way.

Just then a door flew open and I was face to face with Katiana.

Neither one of us reacted.

She simply gave me a nod and kept walking.

What the fuck? She acted like we'd never met. I turned to watch her. She headed down the stairs without turning back around. I tried the handle on the door of the room she'd just left. It opened up to a large bathroom. With two adjoining doors. I tried both doors. They were locked. But I heard something. I pressed my ear to one door and heard some sounds I couldn't quite make out. A deep voice and a higher-pitched one. What sounded like a giggle. And then a protest.

I knocked. Soft at first and then harder.

"Is there somebody in there?"

I still had my ear pressed to the door. The sounds abruptly stopped.

"Hello?" I jiggled the door handle again.

Then as clear as could be I heard a voice. "Go. Away."

I pulled back. I couldn't tell for sure, but the voice sounded familiar. It sounded like a voice I'd heard recently. Not the senator, but someone else.

Then I realized—it was the voice of the senator's crony from the restaurant. The groper.

Just then there was a knock on the bathroom door.

"Just a second," I said.

I hurriedly flushed the toilet and turned the sink on for a second. I flung open the door.

Katiana was standing there.

I raised an eyebrow.

"I think I left my earring on the counter. Excuse me," she said.

I walked out, letting her pass.

She entered the bathroom, and then closed and locked the door.

Earring, my ass.

I pressed my ear against the door.

There was utter silence on the other end.

I imagined her ear pressed against the other side.

I'd wait her out. I wasn't going anywhere. It must've been nearly five minutes before I heard movement. Then a soft knock and I heard her say, "It's me."

I heard a door open and close.

I tried the handle on the bathroom door even though I knew it was locked.

Then I decided to find the adjoining room. To my surprise when I walked down the hall, there was no door to a room. Instead, I was greeted by a blank wall. But something was odd.

I ran my fingers over the wall and found the outline of a door.

That's when I spotted a tiny drop of fresh paint.

They'd walled over a door here. And recently.

Very fucking bizarre.

I had decided I was going to simply sit in the hall until Katiana came back out or someone else did, when a man in a uniform suddenly appeared at the other end of the hall.

"May I help you?" he said stiffly.

"I'm just waiting for the bathroom."

"I will escort you to the guest bathroom downstairs."

"I think I left my earring in this one," I said, thinking, fuck you, Katiana. Two can play this game.

"I assure you, you did not. This bathroom is no longer operational. The hosts would prefer no guests wandering upstairs."

"Oh yeah."

He gave a tight smile. "If you will follow me."

He started toward the stairs.

"I don't think I will."

He gave an alarmed glance back at me.

That's when I heard it. A scream. It was muffled but it was a scream.

I ran toward the bathroom door and started to pound on it. "Do you need help? Is someone in there?"

Then I ran back toward the wall where I'd felt the outline of where a door had been.

"Hello? Do you need help?"

All at once, the hall was filled with men. Secret Service fucks.

"If you'll come with me, Ms. Santella," one of them said.

I felt myself lifted off the ground as four men picked me up.

I was about to fucking throat punch every single one of them when I saw Senator Moore at the end of the hall. She met my eyes and gave me a tiny shake of her head. It was a warning.

"Let go of me," I said calmly. "I didn't realize it was a fucking crime to use the upstairs bathroom."

I shook myself free and marched toward the stairs.

17

I FOUND ANTHONY SURROUNDED BY OLDER, BEJEWELED WOMEN near the pool. He was laughing. If you didn't know him, you'd think he was having the time of his life. But I saw how his eyes kept flicking toward the large French doors leading into the house.

I also saw that when his eyes met mine, his shoulders visibly relaxed.

I smiled and made my way over to him. As I did, I scanned the crowd.

I couldn't find the senator or his intern.

"There you are," Anthony said once I reached the group. "Are you doing okay?" he said leaning down in a quiet voice.

I fluffed my hair. "There was quite a line for John," I said loudly and smiled.

One of the women shot a glance toward the other.

"Oops. I mean the powder room or whatever you ladies like to call it."

I was uncouth. Slightly on purpose. I didn't care. I was annoyed. I was here to support Anthony, but I also had my own agenda. I was going to find out what the fuck Senator Mitchell was up to at this party. I knew what happened at the last party I attended with him. I had my theories. He and his cronies were fucking prostitutes at campaign fundraising parties and at least one had ended up dead.

That server in D.C., Marta, had said they were to ignore screams. that made me think that these men were essentially raping the prostitutes.

I made inane conversation with Anthony's group of ladies for a few minutes until the Senator appeared and once again, pulled Anthony away. Right when she arrived, I saw something in the wooded area. A woman's face had been visible in the thick foliage lining one of the paths leading into a wooded area.

"Madeline wants to speak to us about how we propose to handle the budget for the new bill," Senator Moore said to Anthony.

"Let's go explain it," he said but shot me an apologetic look.

I pushed him towards the senator. "Oh, you must share your ideas with her, Anthony."

He gave me a look showing that he knew I was being fake as fuck.

I couldn't wait for him to leave. As soon as he did, I raced toward the path where I'd seen the woman's face.

She'd had dirty blonde hair. She'd quickly peered out from the wooded area and then disappeared. But for the few seconds I saw her pale round face, I also saw that she had a shiner. One eye was black and blue and nearly swelled shut. I also saw she was holding a pair of heels in one hand. And she looked fucking terrified.

A group of Secret Service men started heading her way and her face disappeared as she dipped back into the foliage.

By the time I was at the path where I'd seen her, the Secret Service men had scattered. Two had gone down the path toward the woods. Two stood on the path looking around.

They hadn't seen her. Thank god.

I sat on a bench and reached down to take off a sandal.

I gave one of the men a bright smile. "My feet are killing me. You guys are so lucky you don't have to wear heels."

They seemed irritated and distracted. Good. I quickly scanned their faces. They weren't the upstairs goons who had accosted me earlier.

One of them spoke into a mic on his shoulder.

"No sign."

"We have her in the alley," I heard a voice say.

They rushed off. I didn't even pause, just stood up and ran after them, holding one of my sandals in my hand, sort of limp running along, trying to stay a little bit behind. They rounded the corner of the house and I paused for a second and followed.

They were tromping through flowerbeds and brushing past tall shrubs. The fucking house was huge. And had odd angles and corners. I hoped we'd get to the alley soon.

Then as I ran faster, taking a second to pull my other high heel off, I caught a glimpse of them ahead. Then I heard a shout and other voices. I raced over to a tall hedge and peered over toward where the voices were coming from. As soon as I had a clear view of the alley, I drew back in horror.

A woman was on the ground. A man above her held a gun with a long silencer.

A small circle of blood bloomed on the woman's torso, seeping through her white dress.

Just then Meg came around the corner. Right when she opened her mouth to scream, one of the goons clamped a hand over it.

18

Before I could react, a black car squealed up and four of the Secret Service men quickly lifted the woman from the ground and threw her in the backseat.

The guy with Meg hustled her into the front seat and then the car was gone.

I blinked.

There wasn't even a speck of blood on the ground where she'd been.

But she'd clearly been dead.

I'd seen her head loll lifelessly to one side as they lifted her. Her open eyes were glassy. A small trickle of blood trailed out of her mouth and down one cheek.

They'd just taken Meg, as well. And I was certain it was against her will.

For a second I froze. But then I realized if they saw me, I would be dead, too.

I began to make my way back toward the party, hugging the thick row of hedges bordering the property. Before long I would be back at the small path that wound through the wooded area to the east of the backyard. Once I was there, I'd be in the clear. Just out for a little stroll.

I could see the path, lit with fairy lights, in front of me, just past one more bend.

Almost there.

The curve of the house momentarily blocked my way. I was about to emerge from behind the structure when I heard a sound. Men's deep voices. Footsteps pounding the pavement.

Then I heard the crunch of leaves as they left the path.

I threw myself on the ground and dropped into a roll, curling underneath the gap between the bottom of the hedge and the lawn.

A split second later, I heard voices close by.

"She went this way."

"Did she see anything?" Senator Mitchell's voice.

"That's unclear, sir."

"Find her. Nobody leaves until she is found."

"Understood."

"Alert me once you find her."

"Yes, sir."

I held my breath as the footsteps crunched past hoping my red dress wouldn't catch their eye if they could see under the hedge or decided to look down.

The men paused.

"I don't think she saw anything."

"That's not up to you to decide."

"Sorry, sir."

Then I heard one man say, "Clear."

I practically wept in relief.

Another man said, "I'll check the alley."

"I'll take the house. Ollie, go tell the valets that nobody leaves."

"Yes, sir."

I waited until it had been silent for at least sixty seconds before I poked my head out. I didn't see a soul.

I quickly got up, brushed myself off and headed back the way I came.

As I got close to the back of the house, I saw a couple clenched in an intimate embrace along the wooded path.

A glass sat on the bench nearby. I scooped it up as I passed.

There were raised voices coming my way. I had the glass up to my lips as three men in dark suits rounded the corner.

They pulled up short when they saw me.

I stumbled a little, spilling my drink.

"Cheers!" I said to them, "You fellows look so handsome in those suits. I wish all men would dress like that."

I slurred my words. I walked straight up to them and reached for one man's sleeve, caressing his arm. The other two men stiffened.

"Oh yes, fine Italian wool. Verrrrry nice."

Then I lost my balance and clutched the other men.

"Shhhhh," I said loudly. "I don't want my boyfriend to hear me saying how handsome you guys look."

I looked around wild-eyed.

"Phew," I said. "I don't think he's around."

Then I pouted. "I went for a walk to see if he'd even notice I'm gone."

"Ms. Santella," one of the men said, clearly tired of my jabbering. "Why don't you come with us?"

I squinted. "Will you take me to him? His name is Anthony. He's the freaking mayor of San Francisco." I giggled. "Like Mayor McCheese but real."

The men had both of my arms. I was starting to become alarmed. My drunk act was not working. They were still going to take me to Senator Mitchell.

They were basically frog marching me away from the party, back toward the driveway. Fuck. Fuck. Fuck.

I didn't want to fight them. If I took them out, which I was fairly certain I could do, it would be game over. The Senator would know I was on to him. It was too soon. I didn't have proof of what he was doing yet. It would be my word against his. And I already knew how that would go.

I needed to outsmart them.

Think, Santella. Think.

If I could somehow convince them to let me back in the house or back at the party, I could create a diversion or find Anthony or someone else familiar.

But I was running out of time. We were nearing the alley where I'd seen the murder.

I was still being supported by two of the men.

The third one was behind us. His voice was low but it carried and I heard him speak to someone or something.

"Target acquired."

Then fate intervened.

Because my head was on one dude's shoulder, not far from his earpiece, I heard the response.

It was the senator's voice. He said one word.

"Terminate."

19

So much for keeping a low profile.

Now it was kill or be killed.

The man supporting me to my left wore his holster on his right.

In other words, it was right within my grasp.

Dumbass.

In my life, it seemed that more than half my battles were won because men underestimated me. Time to make that count.

I slumped just a little more and the man to my left responded exactly as I'd hoped. He adjusted his grip on my back. As he shifted, I lifted the gun out of his unsnapped holster and immediately pressed it into his side.

He stiffened and I straightened up. "Tell your buddy to take out his gun and throw it in the bushes or you're going to get a fucking excruciating side ache in two seconds."

As all this went down, the guy to my right was reaching for his gun. I elbowed him in the jaw in an upper swipe and his head reeled.

It gave me a few seconds advantage.

I sidestepped, keeping the gun stuck into the guy's side and faced the other man. His hand was still going for his gun.

"Tell him," I said, shoving the gun deeper into the man's side.

"Doug. She's going to kill me, man."

The other guy didn't even blink and continued to reach for his gun.

"Not my problem."

He'd just got the words out when the bullet pierced his forehead.

"Jesus Christ," the man beside me said.

I whirled and pointed the gun at him. He held up his hands and was backing up.

"I'm not going to fight you. You're free. Get out of here," he said.

"Here's how it's going to go," I said. "You're going to give me keys to a car and I'm going to drive out of here."

"Whatever you want."

I eyed him. "You're not a Secret Service dude are you?"

He shook his head.

"Who's your boss?"

He swallowed. "I can't tell you."

"Fuck you."

I shot him in the knee.

"The person who hired me will kill me if I tell you."

"I'll kill you if you don't."

I lifted the gun.

He looked down. "You'll kill me. But they will kill me and everyone I love. I'm a father."

"Tell me," I said between clenched teeth.

"You'll have to kill me."

I sighed. I got behind him and prodded him with the gun in his lower back.

"Let's go. Get me a fucking car. Take me where nobody will

see us, too. The second I see someone else, there's a bullet in your back."

He took me around a corner to a long driveway. There was a detached garage some ways from the main house.

About two dozen cars were parked in front of it.

A valet was standing against the garage wall smoking.

As soon as we saw him, the man stopped and stiffened.

"Don't worry. Just act normal and you'll both live."

"You'd kill that kid? You're crazy," the man said in a whining voice.

"You have no idea."

I was bluffing. I wasn't going to kill the valet. Not if I could help it. I really was hoping with all my heart that I didn't have to shoot this guy. A father.

I looped my arm around the guy's waist.

"I'm tired," I said in a low voice. "And you are taking me home. You'll drive us to the entrance to Pebble Beach and then I'll let you out. Understand?"

He nodded.

He reached inside his jacket.

"Easy now."

He extracted a small slip and handed it to the valet.

I kept the gun buried in the small of his back, acting like my arm was around him.

The valet reached into a box set on a table and handed the man a set of keys.

"Can you bring it around for us?" I asked.

The valet nodded. He brought around a four-door black sedan.

I had to separate from the man to get in the car. I wasn't crazy about the idea.

"I'm going to have the gun on you at all times. I can shoot

you dead through the windshield before you can blink. Trust me on this," I whispered in his ear.

I plucked the keys out of the valet's hand at the same time I slipped him some cash. I held my purse with the gun inside pointed at him as I circled around the hood to the passenger door.

Once I was seated beside him, I handed him the keys.

"Let's get the hell out of here."

He paused, his gaze straight ahead.

"I know right now you're weighing your options. You're wondering if I'm going to kill you as soon as we get away from this house. You have no reason to trust me," I said watching the muscle work in his jaw, "But I really don't want to kill you. I want to get out of here and then drop you off safely so you can go home to your family. *Capisce*?"

He nodded and started the ignition, his hands gripping the steering wheel.

I kept the gun in my hand resting on my thigh. I wasn't lying. I didn't want to shoot him.

I would if I had to, though.

"Who was the woman? Why did she get killed?" I said.

"She's a hooker," he said.

I pushed the gun into his ribs. "The correct word is prostitute dipshit."

"She's a prostitute."

"What happened?"

"She was trying to get away."

"Get away?" I said. "What the fuck? She's a prostitute not a prisoner."

He shrugged. "I just keep my mouth shut and do what the boss says."

"There's one more thing you have to tell me if you want to live. Where are they taking the dead woman and the intern?"

He made a grunt.

"You said you want to live, right?"

"You told me all I have to do is drive you out of here."

"And talk."

"I don't know where he lives, but his name is Strauss. He's a doctor."

"That's not going to help the dead woman, is it?" I said. "Why are they taking them to his house?"

"I don't know. He has some connections."

"You do know," I said. "Keep fucking talking."

When we got to the bottom of the drive, the heavy steel gate swung open.

I pressed the butt of the gun into his side.

"Wave nicely at the guard."

He did and I lowered the gun as we pulled onto 17-Mile Drive.

"You're going to have to think hard and talk more," I said. "I'll kill you if you refuse to tell me something that could save that intern's life."

He gave a loud sigh. "I'll tell you what I know, but it's too late for her."

"What are you talking about?"

"As soon as she got into that car they injected something into her neck to kill her. It's too late for her."

The fury rose in my chest and it took all my willpower not to hit the guy in the head with the butt of the gun.

"Why would they take two dead bodies to the doctor?"

"He's a forensic pathologist."

"And?" I was getting tired of fucking around.

I saw a sign for a scenic outlook about a mile down the road. I needed him to talk fast.

"He has access to a crematorium."

"Jesus."

Then we were at the scenic outlook.

"Pull over here."

He did. He parked and put his hands in the air.

I grabbed the keys.

"If all goes well, we get to part company here and you get to find your way home. I need you to carefully get out of the car and go stand with your hands on the hood."

"I don't give a shit about this job," he said. "I just want to get home alive to my family."

"I think we're on the same page, then," I said.

He opened the door and did as I said. I waited and then crawled across the console into the driver's seat. I hadn't checked him for another weapon which was a mistake on my part. But I figured I could get out of his range pretty quickly.

"I want you to keep your hands up and back up until you're against that guardrail."

He did.

There was a small outcropping of bushes right on the other side and then some brush and then the ocean below.

"Hop over the guardrail and just chill there for a second with your hands up in the air," I said. He did.

I gauged the distance. As soon as he lifted one leg over the guardrail, I took off, peeling out, kicking up gravel and dirt. I watched in my rearview mirror as he leapt back over the guardrail.

But he wasn't running toward me. And there was no gunfire.

He hadn't been lying. His family was more important than his job.

Good.

I'd trusted my gut instinct that he was telling the truth and I was glad to see it was still working for me.

As I headed south on 17-mile-drive, away from the gate

where I'd entered the enclave, I rummaged in my bag for my phone.

"Call Anthony."

"Gia?"

"Something's come up. I'll catch up with you later."

"What the hell's going on? People are acting really strange. Senator Mitchell just came up and asked where you were?"

He was whispering.

"The best thing for you is to separate yourself in every possible way from me. Your life depends on it."

"What the?"

I hung up.

20

My next call was to Dante.

"You've got to call off your adoption."

"Good God, Gia, you've got to get help. Go see a therapist. Quit fucking calling me. It's a done deal."

"No!" I shouted.

"Yes. I've already transferred the money into her account. We pick Tana up tomorrow."

"You're fucking kidding?" I said, squealing around a corner. I was nearly to the south gate of Pebble Beach so I pulled over. I'd need a different car if I was going to stay in the gated community.

"She's a killer. They are all killers."

"Gia, I'm going to call your old shrink. Don't call me again until you've had an appointment with him."

"FUCK YOU!" I screeched the words at the phone even though he'd hung up on me. "It's your money. It's your ass. It's your fucking biggest mistake of your life, you pompous prick!"

I felt like crying. But I clenched my fists instead. Fuck him. I had called him because I was going to ask him for help. I was going to tell him what I'd seen and how scared I was that a young woman was going to die and there was nothing I could do about it. But he was done with me.

Dante and I were both Italian so that meant passionate as fuck, but in all our years of friendship, I'd never felt so much anger at him.

I stared at my phone for a second.

"Let it go, Santella," I said aloud, letting the anger seep out of me. I needed my wits about me to find the intern. First I needed to ditch this car.

I pulled into the golf course parking lot, and I dialed Danny in San Francisco.

"Gia!"

"I need an address. A Pebble Beach doctor named Strauss. Also, any crematoriums near him."

"I'm on it. Stand by."

I eyed the cars in the parking lot. There was a beat-up truck with rust and bondo. It was my best bet.

I parked the sedan in a shadowy corner of the lot and headed toward the truck. I could hear Danny through my air pods typing away and humming.

I had hotwired the truck and was leaving the parking lot when Danny spoke next.

"I just texted you the address. The house is about ½ mile from you." Danny had access to my phone's GPS. We'd set it up years ago so he could help me in situations like this

"And," he continued. "There's a funeral home on the other side of 17-mile drive in Pebble Beach called Snyder's and then about two more in Carmel."

"That's a fucking lot of crematoriums for a small peninsula."

"You know what they say about Monterey: for the newly wed and the nearly dead."

I croaked out a small laugh. "That's what we said growing up, how do you know that?"

"I have my ways."

"Thanks, Big D," I said.

I hung up and looked down at the map on my phone. I pulled up a satellite image.

If I took a different road, I could park near the house's backyard and possibly sneak in that way.

That would be my best bet.

21

The doctor's backyard was dense with brush and bordered by the tall Eucalyptus trees so common in my hometown. I remember playing in a backyard with them as children and a friend's mother lost her shit because a classmate had been killed when a large branch fell on him.

Ever since then, I looked at the tall trees with both awe and trepidation.

Now, I was thrilled they provided some cover.

I stood under their shadows and scanned the stone house before me.

A large shimmering turquoise pool lay between me and the house itself.

The windows were all lit up and there were no curtains.

Thank you, Dr. Strauss.

I saw him go from one room to the other. He was gray-haired and slim and wore a form fitting athletic-type black shirt and black joggers. It took me a minute to realize he was on the phone. I saw his mouth moving and he was gesticulating and pacing. Using my phone camera I zoomed in and saw he had air pods in his ears.

He ran one hand through his hair. Then a woman entered the room.

I froze.

She wore a silky nightgown.

He turned and scowled at her and she gave him the finger.

I nearly laughed out loud.

Then she was in his face screaming. He stormed out of my sight.

Within a few seconds he was out on the patio. I held my breath and shrank deeper into the bushes. He paced the side of the pool.

"It will take me a while to access the drugs," he said, his voice carrying across the pool. "If you want it to look like an accident, it will take me a few hours. If you want it to look like an overdose, I can make it happen within the hour. Your call."

He nodded, listening to the person on the other end.

"Guila is already suspicious. She saw the girl. I can't do this anymore if you are going to turn up at my house in the middle of the night with your victims."

He continued. "The money means nothing. You know that. Why don't you just call it what it is? It's blackmailing you bastard. Plain and simple. Don't act like I'm working for you."

He was quiet for a minute and then said, "I'll be there in twenty."

He disappeared in the house.

Now, I raced back toward the car. I needed to follow him wherever he was going.

Back on the road, I found a place near his driveway where I could park without being too conspicuous and wait for his car to emerge. I would follow him without headlights for as long as I could. It would be the only way I would be able to do so undetected on this quiet, narrow road.

Five minutes after I parked, a sleek low-profile Porsche

pulled out of the driveway and without even pausing, careened onto the road. Right fucking toward me. I sunk deep into my seat, holding my breath that he hadn't seen me. I waited a beat and then whipped a U-turn and sped after him. I caught up within a few seconds and kept as far back as I could while still seeing his tail lights. The slight cast of the moon allowed me to see the road without headlights on, but I found myself leaning forward, clenching the steering wheel and peering out the windshield.

We were heading toward the crematorium that Danny had told me about. But then we blew right past it. About a mile later, his tail lights glowed as he slammed on his brakes and swerved down another road. I took the corner a little too fast but managed to correct my steering without going off road or flipping. Thank God for that Skip Barber racing class my dad made me take as a kid at Laguna Seca.

Then the doctor pulled up to a small strip mall and parked. There were no other cars in the parking lot. I slowed and turned on my lights. I drove right past—just another car driving by. I took the first left and found an alley for the strip mall.

I parked and crept toward the back of the store. The doctor's car was parked in front.

I'd just peeked around the side of the building only to see that the car was gone. The lot was empty.

I was just about to turn around when I sensed someone behind me.

Too late.

"Freeze!" I heard two voices shout.

Cops

Before I turned, while I was still in the shadows, I punched a number on my phone.

It was risky as fuck, but might just save my life.

"Hands up!" one said.

"Turn the fuck around. Hands in the air or you get a bullet in your back," the other said.

I thrust my hands up in the air. My right hand held my phone.

"I don't want to drop my phone and crack the screen," I said. "At least let me set it down gently."

I knew it was a risk. They could shoot me and say they thought it was a weapon.

But it was my only play.

When I turned, I faced two uniformed officers with legs spread-eagled and two guns pointing at me.

22

"Set your phone down on the ground. Slowly."

I leaned over and carefully placed it on the cement between us.

"What's the problem officers?"

Of course I knew before they spoke

The doctor got wind that I was following him and pulled over into this strip mall to trap me. Monterey Peninsula police have nothing better to do so they were here in seconds.

I supposed I should be grateful the doctor called the police and not another hitman.

I guess tonight they had enough dead bodies to deal with.

"We had a call about the alarm going off here," one said, keeping his gun trained on me.

The other walked behind me and pulled my hands behind my back to cuff me.

"You probably shouldn't do that," I said.

"Do what?"

"Cuff me."

"Fuck off cunt."

"Save your breath. We all know you're both on the doc's payroll," I said.

"Anything you say will be held against you." *Blah blah blah*, I thought as the cop cuffed me and read me my Miranda Rights.

"I only have two words for you, sailor," I said. "Sal Maffucci."

He was the most high-powered attorney on the Peninsula. His name was tied to kick ass. He had managed to get some of the most notorious mafia members off on what should have been open-and-shut cases. Despite this, he was an upright, upstanding guy.

He'd been my attorney since I was a teenager. I'd inherited him from my parents.

Calling him was my way of making sure crooked cops didn't fucking shoot me right then. Or if they did that they would pay dearly for it.

"Who's that? Your boyfriend?" the other cop said.

"Don't play dumb," I said. "He's going to make sure you guys follow the letter of the law. He's meeting us at the station in a few minutes."

I saw the two cops exchange a look. That's when I knew. They weren't taking me to any police station to book.

"Oh yeah," one cop said. "How's he gonna do that?"

"Drive there the same as you are going to do," a voice said. It came from my phone on the ground.

The police looked down to see Sal's face on my screen.

He waved at them.

"Good evening, officers."

―――

AFTER HE TOLD them he had recorded the entire conversation, Sal said they needed to hand me my phone and allow me to keep him on Facetime as we drove to the station.

One of the cops swore and immediately disappeared. I saw him in the shadows talking on a cell phone as the other cop stuffed me in the back of the squad car. He threw my phone onto the seat beside me.

Finally, the other cop came back and they went off and talked nearby. The door was closed so I couldn't hear them.

"Thanks, Sal," I said. "I think they had other plans besides taking me to the station."

"Careful what you say," he said. "I'm recording you, but they might be, as well."

"I need to warn you,' I said. "This is something big. It goes way beyond a corrupt doctor and crooked local cops."

"Fair enough. See you soon."

When we got to the station, Sal was waiting.

They walked me past him to a holding cell.

He raised his eyebrow and said, "Give me five minutes. The chief is calling me back."

It was less than five minutes when the door to my holding cell opened. Another uniformed cop stood there.

"You pissed off the wrong people, didn't you?" she said. "Luckily the chief isn't a big fan of Tweedle Dee and Tweedle Dum out there so you are getting cut loose."

She undid my handcuffs.

"Thanks," I said, rubbing my sore wrists.

I smiled at her. She began to smile back when the deafening sounds of gunfire filled the air and she fell forward into my arms. I reached out to catch her but she was dead before I could stop her from hitting the floor. I gasped and when I looked up, there was a gun inches away from my face.

"Easy, bitch." It was one of the officers who'd brought me in. "Come on now."

He got behind me and held the gun in the small of my back. He led me to the small lobby. There were two desks and a high counter. A half-eaten salad was on the countertop. Beets and walnuts over spring greens. A magazine lay open near it. A parenting magazine. A slim gold lipstick canister sat near it. It all belonged to that woman cop.

Seeing all this strengthened my resolve to make every corrupt cop in this station pay.

But then the wind was sucked out of me when we got to the lobby and saw Sal.

It was their trump card.

The other cop was holding a gun to Sal's temple.

"It's okay," I told him. 'We'll just do exactly what they say."

His eyes were steely. "I'm not afraid."

"Here's what you're gonna do," the cop near Sal said to me.

'See that little gun there on the counter?" he pointed. "You're gonna pick it up and grip it. Put your hand on the trigger, but don't even think about pulling the trigger because the chamber is empty.

I glanced at his hands. He had on gloves. Out of the corner of my eye I saw that the cop holding a gun on my hand also had gloves on.

Fuck. They were going to frame me for killing the female cop.

"Do it now or your buddy dies. We have no beef with him. Just you."

"Don't do it, Gia," Sal said. "We're both dead anyway."

I shook my head. "I have to. They just want me. They can have me."

I walked over and picked up the gun, closed my eyes and held it in my grip with my finger on the trigger.

"Now, Gia!" Sal shouted.

I wasn't sure what he was doing, but I felt the pressure of the gun pressed against me suddenly gone. I whirled holding the small gun in my hand at the same time I heard another gunshot.

I screamed and pulled the trigger, praying they had lied, but nothing happened. The chamber was empty. I let the gun fall to the floor as I saw Sal on the ground. Dead with a bullet hole in his forehead.

The cop who had been holding him was also crumpled on the ground.

A shiny letter opener stuck out of his neck.

Sal was a *paesano*, Italian by birth. He probably knew a million ways to kill simply from growing up in the old country. And he did it for me, sacrificing his own life. I howled in rage and anger and whirled to face the cop who had been holding the gun on me. He was the fucker who had shot Sal.

His hand was still outstretched with the gun, shaking. He looked surprised and upset that he had killed Sal. Too bad. He was still a dead man.

I nabbed the fork out of the salad on the counter and bolted toward the cop.

It seemed as if it took him great effort to raise his eyes from the dead bodies on the ground and clock me coming at him.

He raised his gun in time for my round kick to come down on his wrist. The blow caused him to release his grip on the gun and sent it scuttling across the tile floor. He stumbled backward.

Out of my reach, but that was okay. Now I was within striking range. He stuck up his other arm as if to ward off a blow to his solar plexus, but I was aiming much higher.

Using a nearby chair, I stepped up quickly and then launched through the air, my arm with the fork outstretched toward his face. At first I thought my aim was off, but at the last second I lowered my arm slightly and the fork met its mark. Right in his eyeball. But not deep enough.

With a roar, he reached to pluck the fork out of his eye. At the same time, I reached up to try to stop his arm from getting to the fork first.

The force of my attack had caused me to slam into him so we were basically pressed up against one another. I had a death grip on his hairy arm reaching for the fork handle. It took everything I had to pull his hand away from the fork and I was losing traction. He took his other arm and began pummeling the top of my head with his fist. I pressed my face even closer to his chest to thwart the blows, but I was still getting slammed pretty good.

We were like two boxers who were clinging close to one another to prevent any decent punches. Except the other boxer had a fork sticking out of his eye.

But this wasn't ESPN boxing, this was some MMA motherfucking shit, so I let my body grow limp and slid out of his grasp only to come right back up with a knee to his groin. He instinctively crumpled. His head dipped long enough for me to lift my upper thigh right into his face. The blow pushed the fork the extra few inches it needed to penetrate his brain.

I sidestepped as he fell with a heavy thud to the floor. He wouldn't be killing anyone ever again.

23

Catching my breath, I stood panting, looking at the carnage around me.

I spotted my small purse on a desk behind the counter and scooped it up along with the cop's gun that was on the floor nearby.

I stepped over bodies and made my way to Sal's still form. His briefcase was on the ground beside him. With a sob, I knelt down and clicked it open. Inside were some papers and car keys. I grabbed the keys and raced out to the parking lot.

Glancing around I clicked the button for the alarm. The lights flashed on a large Mercedes. I'd been hoping he had driven his prized vintage Aston Martin. The Mercedes would be clunky in a pursuit. And from the distant sound of sirens, I might be in one soon.

That's when I saw the motorcycle.

There were five dead people inside and only four vehicles parked out front.

Someone inside had ridden the motorcycle to work.

I raced back into the station and leaned over to search the nearest dead cop's pockets for keys.

Nothing.

I searched the second cop, flipping him over onto his side to get to his pockets.

Jackpot. At the last second, I yanked a leather jacket that was hanging off the back of a chair and pulled that on over my silky dress.

As I raced outside and hopped on the bike, yanking on the helmet I found on the backseat, I heard the sirens suddenly stop. At first I thought it was the helmet silencing the sounds but then I saw two squad cars pull into the parking lot of the station, completely ignoring me zooming across the lot toward the back of the station.

I soon figured out why. They had someone else to deal with me.

Because as I peeled out of the parking lot, two SUV's squealed out onto the road behind me.

The closest one to me was a Porsche Turbo GT. It probably had the sport package. Another SUV was behind it that I couldn't make out.

I'd driven that model Porsche before. It could go 0 to 60 mph in three seconds.

It could hit a top speed of 186 mph.

Thank God I'd ditched the Mercedes for the crotch rocket.

I couldn't tell what type of car the second vehicle was—it was just a lump of black with headlights.

I gunned the motorcycle, leaning into each curve, remembering how it felt to make a bike an extension of my own body, feeling it move underneath me as I shifted.

Whoever was driving the Porsche knew what they were doing because the vehicle stayed close to my tail as I headed south and out of town toward Big Sur.

Soon, I'd left Carmel behind and was zipping down the dark highway with the ocean to my right and lush pastures to my left.

The damn SUV was still behind me. Far enough for me to lose on a curve, but then it was right behind me again on the straightaway. In the far distance, the other SUV hung back.

I'd yanked my dress up to my knees and the extra fabric blew in the wind behind me.

I shivered, suddenly wishing I had leather pants to go with my leather motorcycle jacket.

At first the adrenaline had kept me from noticing the biting wind, but now I was shivering uncontrollably. Even though I had the visor down on the helmet, tears still streamed from my eyes from the wind that had slipped inside.

Then we were at the most treacherous stretch of Highway 1, hugging the cliffs with a steep drop to the ocean hundreds of feet below.

At one point, I had to slow down to make a series of deadly S curves.

It gave both SUV's time to catch up with me. I swore.

I should've been able to navigate the turns as fast as they had, but my entire body was shaking madly now, chilled to the bone and it took all my effort to hang onto the bike handles.

I was losing ground.

If they caught me, I was dead.

If I died, nobody could avenge the deaths these bastards had engineered.

The prostitute. Maybe the intern. The nice female cop. Sal.

Fury filled me and warmed me.

I was not going to give up without the fight of my life.

I readjusted my grip on the bike handles and told myself that the icy wind and chill in my blood was energizing and invigorating.

It fueled me.

Within seconds of thinking this, I no longer felt cold.

I felt fearless and unstoppable.

24

My thighs hugged the sides of the bike like it was part of me as I leaned into the curve, my headlight skittering across the steep cliff to my left and then shooting out into the dark night sky as I straightened the bike out.

I quickly glanced into my rearview mirror to see if I could glimpse headlights behind me.

Two vehicles were back there trying to catch up but now the mirror only reflected blackness.

My hands gripped the handles of the bike as I curled into the next bend of the road.

A narrow strip of dusty dirt shoulder on the right was all that separated the roadway—and me—from a deadly plunge to the crashing waves of the Pacific Ocean below.

At some points, the road perched hundreds of feet above the Pacific Ocean on this winding stretch of Pacific Coast Highway between Monterey and Big Sur.

At least once a year some hapless motorist plunges to their death.

When I was young and had just completed the racing course

at Laguna Seca, I used to sneak out at night just to drive this road. I would take the top off my mother's Fiat and would crank Metallica as I raced down PCH with my hair blowing in the wind feeling death at my shoulder and knowing that even the slightest miscalculation would send me plummeting to my death.

I was young and immortal. Living on the edge, pushing the envelope was the only way I knew how to deal with the turmoil of my emotions at the time.

It all seemed so dramatic at the time.

I'd been so clueless.

This was before I was raped.

This was before my parents were murdered.

This was before I'd been forced to become a killer myself.

I'd navigated these curves dozens of times. I had fucking haunted this road in my youth.

Now, there was a glittering in my side mirror and I could see the Porsche SUV headlights coming up fast behind me.

Go ahead and try to take me out here, you bastards.

The Porsche was fast, but it was no match for the crotch rocket between my legs.

It had been a long time and I was a lot older, but I was confident as I took the curves at speeds that caused me to lean so far that my thighs nearly brushed the pavement.

The headlights grew closer.

The sound of gunshots ripped through the night air. Sparks flew off the pavement to my left as I slipped around another corner.

Motherfuckers.

Adrenaline surged through my body.

I knew there was about another mile of curves before the road leveled out for a stretch as it cut through Big Sur.

They might catch up on the straightaways. I wanted to put some ground between us before then, since I had no protection from gunfire on the bike. I was an easy target.

So far, the road had been empty except for me and the two SUV's chasing me.

Everyone else was home tucked into their beds.

In another two hours, the Monterey Peninsula would be busy with vehicles of those who started their work days before the sun rose—the hotel maids, the gardeners and restaurant workers.

All the hardworking people in the service industry who catered to the rich tourists who kept the Peninsula economy flourishing.

But right now the road was ours and ours alone.

The way I figured it, we were about halfway to the flat stretch of the Big Sur town area.

I saw the headlights of the Porsche bouncing off my mirror at the same time I heard gunshots again.

Damn it. I crouched lower on the bike. They were catching up.

One of the trickiest curves was coming up. A hairpin turn with yellow warning signs. I knew I was going much too fast for it. I'd have to slow down. But if I did, the car would be right on my ass. The bullets were coming too close as it was.

Then the hairpin was upon me. With my thighs gripping the bike and my hands curled and clenched around the handles of the bike I leaned forward to become more aerodynamic at the same time I eased up on the throttle.

As I did, I was suddenly blinded by the headlights of a huge vehicle rounding the corner before me. In my lane. At the same time, my mirror reflected the headlights of the Porsche, which had caught up to me when I slowed down.

I had about two seconds to decide what to do.

And then realized there was no decision to make.

I laid the bike down.

There was a tremendous metal crunching sound and then everything went black.

25

Somewhere in the air, my body and the bike separated and I heard the bike crashing into something before I landed in a tangle of thick brush. I rolled down the steep hill for a few feet before I realized what was happening and began to reach for anything I could grab ahold of. I grasped a handful of bush but it slipped through my hands, slicing my palm as it did. My next attempt worked and I clutched a branch for dear life. My grasp began to slip but then I reached up with my other hand and with both hands holding on, managed to stop my slide down the cliff.

Once I stopped, I felt another large bush at my feet. My feet and bare legs stung like hell as I pulled myself to standing. I unstrapped my helmet and set it down as I took in my surroundings in the dim moonlight. The cliffside was covered with bushes and wasn't as steep as I'd thought. It was steep but I could climb it if I were careful. Every part of my body screamed with pain. Distantly I noted that my limbs felt like they were being devoured by fire ants. I was sure any exposed skin had been scraped raw. As I climbed, my left ankle screamed in pain.

On that same leg, I could feel the blood seeping down my

thigh. Road rash. Maybe so bad I'd filleted my skin. By biting my lip against the pain and pulling myself up branch by branch, I finally got to the road.

The Porsche was flipped and crushed against a pick-up truck. I saw airbags and blood and limbs hanging out of both vehicles. Then I heard a sound.

Beyond the flipped Porsche was the other SUV. It was pulled over to the side of the road.

Someone was standing in the dark beside it speaking.

I kept to the shadows and crept closer.

"Off the cliff. Brody's dead. What do you want me to do?"

He was quiet for a moment.

Idiot had left the driver's door wide open and the vehicle running.

"I saw her bike go off the cliff."

I held my breath hoping he didn't see me creeping closer.

"I told you that there's no way she survived. I saw her lay the bike down."

I froze.

"Fine," he said and then I saw him stick his phone in his pocket.

"Jeezus. He wants a photo of a dead girl? How in the fuck am I supposed to get one? Crawl down the goddamn cliff?"

He started toward the area where my bike had gone off the side.

I held my breath as he passed me crouched in the dark.

As soon as he was a few feet past me, I raced toward the driver's side door. As I did, I passed into the road and in front of the lights. As my shadow blocked out the headlights for a second, he swore and turned around but I was already in the driver's seat. I slammed and locked the door and then gunned the engine as he raced toward me.

"Chicken. You're it," I said.

At the last second, he dove out of the way.

"Good choice."

I would've run him down without a second thought.

I gunned the engine and drove as fast as I could, only slowing down for the hairpin turns and keeping an eye on my dark rearview mirror. There weren't any headlights behind me, but that didn't mean anything.

I wasn't so foolish as to think that guy who had dove out of the way wasn't calling someone else to come after me.

Finally, I was down on the flat stretch of road through Big Sur. I ripped through town ignoring the lowered speed limit, counting on all the sleepy deputies to be somewhere else.

Then I was south of the famed town and driving past the road that led to where Henry Miller had lived. Soon I passed the Henry Miller library and the Esalen Institute for holistic something or other, and then had a fairly straight shot. I headed to San Simeon, where the famed Hearst Castle was.

I'd gone on a school field trip when I was in high school and we toured there as part of our film unit after watching Citizen Kane

The ridiculously opulent house and grounds still had wild animals roaming the property at the time. I remember seeing zebra, elk and bison. The zoo with giraffes, lions, bears and kangaroo had been dismantled before my parents were born.

As soon as I got to the town, I'd ditch the vehicle and check into an obscure motel for the night before I decided what to do next.

I had a little more than an hour of driving.

With the heater cranked, my chills eventually went away.

I didn't dare slow down, but whenever there was a straight-away I took one hand off the wheel and searched the vehicle with my other one, feeling around in the dark.

By reaching behind me, I found a case of bottled water and

eagerly cracked one open, gulping it so fast that the water dripped down my face. Also in the back was a small, insulated lunch container. I ripped it open. There was a little note on top of the neatly packaged food. All I saw by the light of the dashboard was a small heart and name. I wadded it up and tossed it in the back seat behind me.

"Looks like wifey packed a lunch for the assassin before his busy night," I said, wolfing down a ham and cheese sandwich and some grapes.

The sun was just starting to poke above the rolling hills to my left when I pulled into San Simeon and examined my face in the rearview mirror.

Not too bad. Thank God for the helmet.

I pulled the SUV behind the motel near a line of trees.

I searched the back of the SUV and found a first aid kit along with some jumper cables and other emergency supplies that wifey had probably bought for Christmas. It all looked brand new. I stuffed the first aid kit into the plastic bag.

I wasn't sure how to hide my ripped dress and bloodied leg. I then eyed a blanket that was also in the back. I wrapped it around me like a long skirt and decided that my makeshift outfit would have to do.

26

Luckily, the old man at the Silver Surfer Motel was more interested in my boobs hanging out of my ripped dress than the state of the dress itself. I dug around for some cash in my bag and slid it across the counter. He leered and handed me the key.

Right after I let myself in my room, I heard the sound of someone arguing. I peered out the curtains on my front window and saw an older couple leaving a room nearby. They were dressed in shorts and windbreakers. They were arguing over something. They had a map they were holding out. But they didn't have luggage. I took in the woman's size. She would do. I watched until they had gone down the stairs and got into a small sedan. Once they had driven out of the parking lot I rushed over to their room. I picked the lock with one of the heavy duty paperclips I kept in my purse at all times and headed to the bathroom closet. I grabbed a pair of black travel pants and a white tee-shirt, and some toothpaste and shampoo.

There was a bottle of vodka in the mini fridge so I nabbed that and an apple.

Back in my room, I stripped down and stepped into the shower wincing as the water pelted my sore and cut body. My thigh was raw with road rash. I took the motel soap bar and grimaced as I washed out each and every cut.

Luckily nothing was very deep. The shower water ran pink as the blood washed down my legs.

The helmet had saved my face—and life probably.

After my shower, I dressed as many wounds as I could with the meager supplies in the first aid kit and put on the black pants and white shirt and then put the leather jacket back on. I was warmer but couldn't fully beat the chill I had from earlier in the night.

I popped open the vodka and downed it as I munched on the apple, flipping on the TV to see if there was any mention of the missing intern.

I froze when the first image I saw was of Anthony.

It was a morning news show and they had cut off for breaking news.

He was leaving the party surrounded by journalists thrusting microphones at him.

His tie was undone and his face was white. It said the footage was from yesterday.

I listened in shock as the reporters shouted questions to him.

"Is it true your girlfriend is wanted for murder?"

"No comment."

"Mayor Ferraro, do you have plans to resign now that the Senator has withdrawn his backing of you?"

I gaped at the TV screen.

"No comment," he said again.

Then the footage went back to the talking heads in the newsroom.

"What a wild story," one woman with a light brown helmet said.

"No kidding," a pretty boy reporter said. "She doesn't look the type."

Then there was a photo of me. I was in a black leather dress at the recent fundraiser for the hotel.

"Sometimes people just snap though," the woman said.

"Also, she does have that Mexican drug cartel connection," he said.

Then the fucking weather man decided to add his two fucking cents.

"From what Ken was saying earlier, there is a criminal history there. This isn't the first time Gia Santella has been looked at for murder."

"What?" Helmet Head said.

"We have reporters working on it right now, we'll be updating this story throughout the day."

The scrolling text at the bottom of the screen said, "Breaking News. San Francisco Mayor's Girlfriend wanted for murder spree."

I closed my eyes.

Fuckity Fuck.

This was bad.

Really bad.

"Meredith, we're going to go live. The mayor is making an announcement."

Then the footage cut to an area of Carmel where the ocean and golf course showed in the background.

Anthony was dressed in a suit and freshly shaven. The only indication that he was under stress was a slight shadow under his eyes.

"Thank you all for being here today. I'm going to make a brief statement and will not be taking questions."

The reporters were already shouting and going crazy.

Anthony paused, a beacon of patience until everyone shut the fuck up.

"I was with Gia Santella most of the night. I know she's innocent of these crimes. I am not going to rest until I've proven that and held whomever is responsible accountable for these atrocious crimes. We will get to the bottom of this."

Then he stepped away.

After a few seconds, the TV flashed back to the station.

"So he's not even going to answer questions about resigning?"

"It's a pretty clear statement that nobody else believes the mayor if the senator has withdrawn his support of the mayor's campaign," Helmet Head said.

"He's taking a huge risk defending a killer," another reporter responded.

"Yeah, I hate to say it but I think this is the end of Mayor Anthony's Ferarro's political career."

"It's too bad, really. He's done a good job and I think he would have made a good senator."

Then they cut to the artichoke festival.

I stared at the TV.

"I'll fix this," I said to the empty room. "I promise."

27

I'd fallen asleep with the TV droning in the background and woke up with a start.

I sat up trying to figure out what had awoken me in such a state of pure panic.

That's when I heard them, sirens in the distance.

I closed my eyes.

Maybe the sirens weren't for me.

Maybe.

I reached for the gun on the nightstand and tucked it into the back waistband of my pants and then looped my crossbody bag over me. I stood with my ear to the door, listening. I couldn't hear anything outside. I pulled back the curtain a fraction. It was dark. I'd slept all day.

I saw two cars in the parking lot. Nothing to be alarmed about.

The sirens grew louder and closer.

I reached for the door handle contemplating a run for it when an ambulance went racing by on the road in front of the motel.

My shoulders sagged in relief.

Either way, it was time to go.

I'd hotwire one of the beat-up sedans out front and then trade it in when I got to the more populated San Luis Obispo area. There was a college there and lots of people and places where I could blend in while I figured out what to do next.

I needed to somehow prove that Senator Mitchell had killed those people.

I turned the door handle and cracked the door. As I opened it, a large black gun was thrust into the narrow space, right in my face, squashing my nose.

I tried to slam the door on the gun but a foot was already jammed in the door.

The next thing I knew the door had been slammed open and the last thing I saw was the gun coming down on my head.

―――

I OPENED my eyes and blinked. Within seconds I remembered what had happened and struggled to sit up.

There was a bright light shining in my eyes. I blinked until my vision could focus. I was in a very well appointed bedroom. The walls had velvet red and gold patterned wallpaper. There was a gold and crystal bedside lamp. The bed underneath me was plush and absorbed my beaten body. I lifted my head as far as I could to take in my surroundings.

My arms were stretched out above my head and my hands were tied to a gold headboard. My feet were bound together at the foot of the bed and then tied to the gold footboard.

As I twisted to look around the room, I turned to my right and saw the senator watching me with a calm look on his face. He was seated in an upholstered antique chair. He was leaning forward, his elbows on his knees.

"Do you like this place? It's one of my favorite vacation homes," he said. "Did you know it used to be owned by Clint Eastwood? He was the one who inspired me to go into politics. He was a movie star and a mayor. I wanted his life. That's why I bought this house as soon as it went on the market. It was where he lived. Unlike you, I wasn't born into money. I had to work for it. So you are in no position to judge me for what I've done to create the life of my dreams."

"Your dream life is killing innocent young women? Classy." I said to stall, but I was thinking. Clint Eastwood. We were back on the Monterey Peninsula. Probably in Carmel. I think that's where Eastwood had his home when he lived here.

"You're very interesting, Gia Santella."

"Fuck off."

"If the matter wasn't so urgent, I'd keep you around for a while, like I did with Meg. I really needed her the last two nights to get through this. She was so helpful. She really helped me relieve a lot of the stress I had about the mess you caused."

"If you touched her..." I hissed and struggled uselessly against the ties binding my hands and feet.

"Oh, I touched her alright."

"You're a monster."

"Gia, she wanted it. I know you saw it the other night. I saw you watching us. She loved me. I only gave her what she needed and wanted to be fulfilled."

Rage surged through me.

"Where is she?"

He frowned and then exaggeratedly shook his sleeve to reveal his watch. He peered down at it.

"Probably by now she's going into the fire. She'll be a little pile of bones and dust soon. Don't worry, she's so drugged that she shouldn't feel any pain. Probably thinks she's lying on the beach somewhere getting a nice tan. I'm not a sadist. I don't enjoy torturing people."

"That's not what the dead prostitute in Washington, D.C. would say. I saw her neck."

He smiled. "I know you did. That's why you're going to commit suicide. It will be obvious why you did it—you felt so guilty about your crime spree. But first we need the final touch."

He stood up and walked toward the closed bedroom door.

Despite myself, I felt a pit of dread in my stomach. What fucking final touch?

He opened the door. I strained to see but could only see shadows outside the room. He said something in a low voice and then a man I'd never seen before came into the room. He was wearing black gloves and holding my dagger. The dagger I'd left in my hotel room in San Francisco. It was a specially designed one from Sicily. A gift from Eva many years before.

A man in nurse's scrubs followed. He held a tray with a syringe and small vials. Fuck me.

"We can do this two ways, Gia. You can either put your hand on the knife willingly or Sergio here will give you a little poke that will paralyze you and then we will wrap your fingers around the dagger without your help. You decide."

I glared at him. "I'll do it."

"Good girl."

I closed my eyes for a brief second, imagining the feel of my dagger in my grip. They were fools to even let me within a few feet of it. But then I remembered how tightly my wrists and feet were bound.

Still. It meant a weapon within my reach.

The dude with the crew cut walked on one side of the bed. The nurse came to the other side and set the tray down on the nightstand. He looked at the Senator who nodded.

"I don't want to say I don't trust you, but I don't trust you. So Sergio is going to be waiting here in case you think you can fight this. I'm warning you that once that needle is in your neck you'll have about two seconds that will be the last two seconds you'll ever be able to move willingly in your life. It will paralyze you but you will be aware of everything going on. You, unlike, my dear Meg, will be perfectly aware of being put into the fire but unable to do a damn thing about it. Are we clear?"

I gritted my teeth and nodded.

He looked at the crewcut guy and the guy placed the handle of the dagger in my palm.

"Now, squeeze tightly."

I did and it took all my willpower not to thrust the blade a few inches up into the tender, exposed wrist of the bodyguard.

As soon as I thought that, he reached down and, grasping the handle at the very tip, took it away from me.

I wondered if I'd just blown my one shot at survival. But there was no mistaking Sergio hovering over my left side with a syringe ready to go.

From my peripheral vision, I could see him put the syringe back on the tray.

The senator cleared his throat.

"Okay," he said in a loud voice. The door opened and two men came in holding Blondie up on each side.

Her hair was tangled and her dress ripped. Her eyes blackened. Her lips were swollen.

As soon as they had stepped into the room, the crew cut body guard walked over to her. He took my dagger and with one swift thrust, plunged it into her stomach and up. She gasped. He withdrew my bloody dagger and then plunged it again, higher this time. I knew that it had hit its mark. I'd been staring right into her eyes and I saw the second the life left them. The two men on each side of her let go unceremonious and she fell in a heap onto the ground.

I swallowed and gritted my teeth.

The two men each took knives out and started walking toward me.

I knew what was next.

28

To my surprise, when the two men reached me, one on each side of the bed, they sliced the ties binding my wrists. The man who killed Blondie, Sergio, walked to the foot of the bed and using his own knife, cut through the ties on my ankle.

"Call them now," the senator said to Sergio, who left the room, evening the odds a bit.

As soon as my ankles were also free, I put my palms down and pulled myself to a sitting position, drawing my legs up.

"Easy now," the senator said as I sat up.

I rubbed my wrists to stall. I was gauging how far away the syringe was on the nightstand and how long it would take me to grab it and stick the closest person. None of the men had guns just those stupid little knives that they had already put back in their sheaths. Morons.

The nurse wasn't a threat and I really hoped I wouldn't have to kill him. But I would if I needed to.

"I thought a lot about how the fearless Gia Santella would kill herself," the Senator said.

"Oh yeah. And what did you come up with?" I asked, thinking, *keep talking, douchebag.* He was a politician after all and his desire to expound on stupid ass things would be his undoing.

"Well, I was just bluffing about the paralyzed slide into the crematorium. That really wouldn't work. It was just a threat to get you to grab your dagger," he said. "What I really needed to do was stage a scene where you killed Katiana and then killed yourself because you're completely surrounded by police and have absolutely no way out."

That must be who Sergio had left to call. He could return any second. He was the biggest threat in the room. These other two men, who stood with their backs to the wall on either side of the bed, looked like Secret Service. They could be dangerous to some people, but not me.

"They're on their way. We should be hearing the sirens any second."

"And how will I kill myself," I said, inching closer to the side of the bed with the syringe.

He was about to answer when I made my move. In one swift move, I rolled over and off the bed, landing on my feet, facing the bed with my right hand gripping the syringe and my left hand scooping up the metal tray it was on. I whirled and lunged for the man with the knife who had started toward me with a shout. I stuck the syringe deep into his neck right below his jaw. He fell to the ground as I let go of the syringe still stuck in his neck and gripped the metal tray with both hands and I used it to parry the thrust of the knife from the other man who had surprisingly leaped across the bed with a shout, his knife aiming for my chest.

The knife clunked against the metal tray. He kept at it, though, stabbing at me, but hitting the tray I used as a shield.

In the chaos, I could hear sirens in the distance.

This time when the man with the knife came at me, I sidestepped the blow and he stumbled forward off balance. I reared back and gave a solid kick that landed on his jaw. He was already on the way down when I solidified it by slamming the tray down on the back of his head.

Boom. He hit the ground and didn't move again. His jacket opened revealing a gun in a holster.

I looked up to see the nurse cowered in the corner.

When I turned to confront the senator, he was gone. I leaned over and took the gun out of the man's holster before I jumped over Blondie's body and raced out of the room.

29

The hall led to a loft overlooking the main open space of the house. I saw the Senator tromping down a staircase to the right. At the bottom, he had two choices. If he ran to the left, he could run out the front door. The only thing to his right was a bank of windows with the sliding glass doors open leading to a large wooden deck. That's where I wanted him.

I could probably fire and hit him easily right then, but something stopped me. I wanted more answers. I wanted to find something that would allow me to clear my name.

I leaned over the rail, holding the gun until he reached the last step then I fired just to the left of him. I hit a vase and it shattered. Even so, he started to go left toward the front door so I fired again, this time the bullet whizzed by his arm and hit a picture frame on a table.

He raced to the right and out the sliding glass doors.

"Good boy," I said as I sprinted for the stairs. I took them two at a time keeping my eyes glued on the windows to the deck to make sure he didn't try to sneak back toward the front door.

With the gun in my hand leading, I raced through the open sliding glass doors to the deck, my head swiveling.

I spotted him at one end, tugging to free a poker near a built-in fire surrounded by chairs.

"Drop it!" I shouted.

He looked over at me, his normally coiffed hair askew, his eyes wild.

He straightened and held out his palms to me showing they were empty. It was over.

But then he did something strange, his eyes involuntarily shot to one of the chairs. I followed his gaze. His phone was on the arm of a chair.

He'd probably called for help.

But it was too late.

He was trapped. There was nowhere to go. The ocean lay on the other side of the deck at least fifty feet below. There were solar lights scattered along the deck rails, casting his face in a greenish glow. Beyond him was the night sky with big poofy white clouds being blown around in swirling patterns.

"Put your hands up over your head," I said pointing the gun at him.

He did.

I was going to try not to kill him and to actually call the police to arrest him so he could be charged with all his heinous crimes. "Now back over there."

I watched him scoot over against the rail. The clouds had whipped into a frenzy now out on the water, but it was surprisingly quiet and calm where we were besides the crashing of the waves below. Holding the gun, I came closer.

"Give me one reason not to put a bullet in your head right now."

He smirked and it took all my self-control not to press down on the trigger with my index finger.

"If you kill me, Meg dies."

I froze. "I thought you said she was already dead?"

"She's been drugged. Right before you came out I sent a text telling them if they don't hear from me in the next ten minutes to put her in the fire."

I wanted to pull the trigger so badly my hands were shaking. But not now. He'd played his cards well.

"I'll let you live if you have them bring me Meg."

"It would take too long for them to bring her."

I smiled. "I don't give a fuck how long it takes, have them bring her here to me or you die."

"It won't be possible," he said and shook his head. "The only thing I can do is tell them not to kill her. Bringing her here would be impossible."

"Make it fucking possible. You've set up a situation where I have nothing to lose. You've given me no reason to try to save myself. But you're not a complete idiot," I said. "You know I'll let you live if it means the girl lives, right?"

"As you so eloquently said, I'm not a 'complete idiot' so why would I bring you the girl when holding her life in question is the only thing keeping you from killing me."

"Unlike you, fuck face, I actually keep my word," I said.

He laughed. "You expect me to believe an assassin has a code of honor? Keeps her word?"

I waited until his laughter died down and then I met his eyes. He squirmed and looked away.

I waited.

"Okay," he said.

"Text them now. Hold up your phone to show me what you wrote before you hit send."

He reached down and picked up his phone. He typed for a few seconds and then held the phone up. I moved closer, straining to see the words in the dark. The text said, "Bring the girl to my home. Alone. Do not tell anyone else."

As soon as I read it I backed up, keeping the gun on him.

"Hit send."

He did.

"Put your fucking phone on the ground between us."

He hesitated a second too long so I fired a bullet into the wood near his feet.

He jumped.

"Now."

He moved a few steps forward.

"There."

He crouched and set it down on the ground.

"Now back up."

He did.

"Back up more, away from the fire pit. Up against the rail."

He did. I reached down and scooped up his phone, keeping my eyes glued on him even though I doubted he could possibly be a threat to me.

I walked over so I was near the fire pit circle and he was trapped in the corner of the deck.

"What's your passcode?"

He scowled.

I lifted the gun toward his face. "I said I'd keep my word but only if you do as I say ..."

He reeled off four numbers and I punched them in.

"What are you doing?" he asked.

"Making sure you sent that text."

But I hadn't even looked at the messages. Instead, I brought up the camera's video and hit record. I set the phone down on the Adirondack chair beside me.

"Now what?" he asked. "You kill me?"

"Nah," I said. "Now we wait."

"Can I sit down?"

I shrugged and he slid to the deck with his back against the rails.

"I have a question for you," I said. "Were you always a fucking asshole or did the world of politics corrupt you?"

He gave a snort. "You're worried about your precious Anthony, aren't you?"

I glared.

"Let's just say that I never had the same ideas as Anthony about my political career. I was raised to be President. My father was a senator who failed in his presidential bids and his dream was for me to be the one to achieve his dream."

"Did your dad want you to kill people to achieve that goal?" I said.

The senator was quiet for a minute.

"Times have changed since my dad was in office. It's a lot tougher. There's a lot of pressure. Things work differently."

"Did your dad fuck prostitutes and then kill them for fun like you?"

"That was an accident," the senator said, his voice raising. His face grew red with anger. I saw him clench his fists. Good.

"Was that the first accident you've had? It wasn't, was it?"

He didn't answer.

"What about Meg? You don't seem upset that she was going to die to protect your secrets?"

"I actually am pretty upset about that. Believe it or not I really cared for her. But she found out some things she shouldn't have. I didn't have a choice."

He said it as if Meg wasn't on her way to us right then. It worried me. Had he sent some sort of code to his contacts?

"What about Katiana? You supported her fucked up sex trafficking scheme and killed her to frame me. And what about the other murders you want me to take the fall for?"

"I have a higher purpose," he said. "People who stand in my way are unfortunately sacrificed for the greater good."

"What fucking greater good?" I said, anger flaring through me.

"You don't want to hear this,' he said. "You won't believe it. But I truly want to help our country."

"You're fucking mad."

"I knew you wouldn't believe me."

"How long until your man is going to be here with Meg."

He squinted. "How long has it been?"

I didn't answer. I lifted the gun again.

"Maybe ten more minutes."

I picked up the phone. The recording had been working.

"With Meg's collaboration of what happened and your confession on this phone, I think you might want to give up your dreams of being president."

30

THE SENATOR PUT HIS HEAD IN HIS HANDS.

"It's okay, I'm sure you'll find plenty of new friends in prison," I said. "I mean you're a good-looking guy and all."

His phone buzzed. I glanced down.

There was a text.

"I have the girl."

I hit his passcode and typed, "Bring her in the house. Put her on a couch. Take a picture of her there and then text me when you are back in your car."

My text got a thumbs up and then I waited.

"Looks like your man delivered."

The senator scoffed. "Of course. Everyone does what I say. I mean everyone. You'll find that out soon. You'll be sorry for ever daring to confront me. You think that recording means something? It's going to go away like you will go away. I have friends in very powerful places."

"Hey idiot," I said. "When I hung up I hit record again. And I've already sent both recordings to a Washington Post reporter I know. It's over."

He tried not to react but I saw him chewing on the inside of his cheek working over what I'd said.

A few seconds later, his phone dinged again. I saw a picture of Meg on the couch.

I texted back: "Send me a picture of your face in your vehicle."

I waited and then when I got the photo texted, "Return to the crematorium and wait for my orders."

"Yes, sir."

I'd make sure the cops picked him up there.

I hit speaker and pressed 9-1-1.

"911 what is your emergency?"

"Please help. There are dead bodies everywhere. I'm at Senator Mitchell's house and he's just confessed to killing people. He's restrained right now so he's not a threat, we're Code 4, but I need the police and medics asap. There's a kidnapping victim who needs medical care. Also, one of her kidnappers is going to be at the Snyder crematorium in about 10 minutes."

Then I hung up.

I set the gun down on the arm of the closest Adirondack chair and put the phone beside it.

31

Before I had turned from setting the phone down, the senator made his move.

I whirled in time to see him try to throw himself off the deck.

I hesitated, not sure if I should shoot him, push him, or try to save him.

"Freeze!" a voice said.

Fuck. Not again.

I threw up my hands.

But the two police officers rushed past me and tackled the senator.

Within seconds he was on the deck, face down and cuffed.

I still had my hands in the air when I heard a familiar voice.

"Thank God, you're okay."

Anthony.

"Anthony, son, I'm so relieved you are here. Your girlfriend tried to kill me. She killed Katiana," he said, his face turned sideways from the deck where he lay.

"Mike," Anthony said. "You need help."

"You believe her?" The senator said spluttering. "Over me? Your father's best friend?"

"Were you best friends?" Anthony said squinting. "I never knew you until after he died. You're the one who told me that you were his best friend. My mother said he hated you."

"What? Nonsense. The old woman doesn't know what she's talking about. That's why she's in the rest home."

He had barely completed the words before Anthony stood astride him with his foot pressed on the senator's back.

"Don't you ever call my mother an old woman again," he said, gritting his teeth.

The senator didn't answer. The cops backed up.

Anthony crouched down beside the senator's head. "Do you understand?"

I saw Anthony's knuckles grow white as he clutched his hands into fists. I knew he was exhibiting supreme self control.

"I asked you if you understand?"

The senator nodded.

Then Anthony headed toward me.

The cops came back over and one kicked the senator in the side.

"Oops."

Now, Anthony was in front of me.

"Hey sailor!" I said and couldn't help but grin.

He laughed and drew me in for a hug.

I pulled back. "You defended me. Even knowing it was going to cost you the election?"

"Have we met?" he said. "If you know me, you know that people are more important to me than holding office."

I smiled.

"That's true. I'm sorry I ever doubted you."

He drew back. "You did?"

I felt ashamed, but I nodded. I held up my thumb and index finger in a pinching gesture. "Only this much," I said and winced.

He looked away.

"That really stings," he finally said. "But I guess if I try to see it from your point of view, it makes sense. You thought I was blindly following that fool," he said and gestured toward the Senator. We both looked over. The police had lifted him to his feet and were leading him inside.

I heard a volley of sirens and squealing tires.

"The cavalry's here."

"Oh no! How's Meg?" I started toward the sliding glass doors.

"She's coming around. They were loading her into the ambulance when I came out here. They got here at the same time as us."

"How did you know? To come?"

"A hunch. And knowing the senator pretty well," he said. "I grew up with a guy who is now a cop on the Monterey police force so I reached out to him. We were heading this way when your 911 call came across the radio. We were the closest unit but instead of responding we just decided to get here first in case any of the other cops were on the senator's payroll like the Carmel cops."

"You knew about that?"

"It took me a while, but we figured it out. We have a confidential informant who gave us the names of the bad cops. She said there were at least two Monterey cops in the senator's pocket. That's why we figured he'd stick around in town where he knew he had protection."

"What will happen to Meg?" I said.

"She'll be taken to the Monterey hospital and checked out, but she responded to her name when I first came in."

"Thank God."

I scooped up the senator's phone from the chair and handed it to Anthony.

"There's a recording on here with the senator owning up to

all the evil shit he did," I said. "I told him I'd already sent it to a reporter, but I didn't. Maybe you could do that? It would mean more coming from you?"

Anthony nodded. "Good. We also have the security footage from the house."

I didn't know what he was talking about. He could tell by the look on my face. He pointed and I saw cameras on both ends of the deck.

"His entire house is a Big Brother nightmare. The bedroom, the bathrooms, the showers, all recorded all the time. He bragged about it when I came to stay here. He told me there wasn't an inch of space not recorded except for closets in the guest bedroom, so of course every time I undressed, I did so in the closet. Very awkward."

"The cops know?"

"Yep, I sent them there immediately," He said. "He's got a hidden panic/control room that you can access through his walk-in closet. I'm sure those tapes are not going to help his case, either."

"There's a few bodies in the master bedroom," I said, cringing at how casual it sounded.

Anthony took it in stride. "Well, there's nothing to do about that now, is there?"

I shook my head.

No.

I looked around.

There was nothing else I could do here.

32

I told Anthony I wanted to go to the hospital and see how Meg was doing.

"Let's go."

I followed him into the house.

As I did, a cop drew his weapon.

"Freeze! It's the fugitive!"

I threw up my hands wearily. "Really?"

"She's cool," another cop said. "We've dropped the warrant."

"You sure, Sarge?" the other cop said, his finger twitching on the trigger.

For a second fear raced through me. He was probably on the Senator's payroll.

"Stand down, officer."

The cop lowered his gun.

Meg had her eyes closed when we walked into her hospital room. There was an armed guard stationed outside her door and he was flanked by two Secret Service men.

Anthony said she was a state's witness and would be in protective custody until the Senator's trial was over.

Trial. It was music to my ears.

After we walked in, her eyes fluttered open. They skimmed over me and she frowned.

Then they rested on Anthony.

"Mayor?"

"You're going to be just fine," he said. "The Senator has been arrested. He can never hurt you again."

She gave a wan smile. A tear slid down her cheek.

"I found out what he did. I saw the tapes. They were in his bedroom," she said. "He didn't even try to hide them. When he found out I knew, he turned cold and said it was nice knowing me. He was going to kill me, right?"

I gave a slow nod, watching her. "I'm sorry," I said.

"I'm just so embarrassed. I thought ... I don't know. I guess I was foolish."

"You weren't," I said. "He's a master con artist. One of the best. Which is how he got to where he is. He fooled everyone. But that's all over now."

She smiled and then her eyes grew steely. "I hope he rots in hell."

"With your help and mine, he's going to," I said.

33

Anthony insisted I wear a revealing green dress for his ceremonial swearing in as a new senator.

"The attention really should be on you," I said. I tucked my dagger into my new Chanel crossbody bag. I'd gotten it back from the Monterey police.

"You're bringing your dagger?"

I made a face. "Must I bring up the last time I tried to carry a weapon in my Chanel bag and you promising me I wouldn't need it?"

"Ouch."

"I'm bringing it."

"Of course. Do your thing."

"I will."

We'd been in the Washington, D.C. hotel room for less than an hour.

A car had picked us up at the airport. This time we'd flown commercial.

Senator Mitchell's jet had been confiscated as evidence along with a Ferrari, oodles of cash, gold bars, cell phones, computers, and a veritable chemistry lab of drugs that incapacitated women.

"Let's go," Anthony said.

Because we had flown commercial, our flight had been delayed due to weather and we'd be cutting it close getting to the ceremony.

We'd quickly showered and dressed after we arrived. A car was picking us up in a few minutes.

It didn't stop me from looking at the room's one bed and having my heart pound.

The anticipation of what might happen in that bed later tonight was building.

I wasn't sure I'd ever waited so long to hop in bed with a man I was attracted to. Maybe it was a sign of maturity. Or just bad luck.

Ever since the senator was arrested, it had been a whirlwind of activity. I'd barely seen Anthony.

Anthony had won the election by a landslide as soon as the senator's misdeeds were revealed to the public and Anthony's role in exposing them was known. And, of course, I'd been cleared when all this came out.

There was also going to be a special election. Senator Wendy Moore had been arrested as one of Mitchell's accomplices. She knew all about the sex trafficking and murder that night. Of course.

And come to find out, Blondie and her had been old classmates when they were in high school. Except Blondie had been called Patsy Jackson and had grown up in the same hick town as Wendy. When Wendy made it big as a senator, Patsy had come to town and blackmailed the senator with photos of sex parties and drug use when they were younger.

The senator was arrested and facing a long list of charges

including murder and sex trafficking, extortion, kidnapping, blackmail and more.

He'd been flown to a jail in Washington, D.C. to face trial.

Blondie's involvement had been blown open. She was the groomer. The one who befriended and lured young women to the Senator's circle, where they were usually raped and then turned over to powerful men overseas or made sex slaves in America. When I heard about the date rape drugs I knew that Blondie had spiked the Champagne she'd given me at that first party. It was why three or four drinks had flattened me. She was on to me from day one.

Blondie's adoption scam was also unearthed by a bulldog Washington, D.C. reporter who had toppled a sex trafficking scheme with tendrils reaching into the top echelon of the U.S. military. Her investigation showed that the girls put up for adoption had been sex-trafficked from Afghanistan.

Most of them had been forced to marry older men to escape the country after their parents had been murdered by the Taliban.

Because America wanted to look like heroes, some top government officials had covered up the fact that these children, as young as seven, were arriving on U.S. military bases as "wives" to men as old as seventy-nine. Some of the men had "married" as many as eight girls in polygamous arrangements and basically raped them.

To avoid any scandal, Blondie had worked with the Senator and top military officials to "get rid of the girls" by selling them to those willing to pay a high price for a fast adoption.

Dante and Wayne.

The military official sold the girls to Blondie who then sold them to wealthy families eager to adopt a child. Now, those who had adopted the children were also under investigation.

I wasn't holding my breath waiting for a thank you or

apology from Dante. He was a stubborn fucker, but I knew he would eventually come around.

He wasn't my blood but we were family anyway and I knew it was just a matter of time before we would be good again. At least that's what I told myself every time I thought about calling him and didn't and wanted to cry.

I'd done my part. It was up to him to reach out now.

I'd wanted to call him to ask him what to wear to the swearing in ceremony but ever since our fall out about the adoption, he'd been avoiding my calls. I stopped calling weeks ago.

Instead, I'd called up the Gucci store in San Francisco and asked them to send me ten potential dresses suitable for a senatorial swearing in ceremony. Then I took selfies and sent them to Anthony, who picked the slinky one with the deep cut square neck and the high leg slit. It was sexy as fuck. But I worried it was too sexy. Dante would have picked the perfect dress.

I was putting on black onyx dangling earrings when Anthony came up behind me in the bathroom mirror.

"You are ravishing." He leaned down and kissed my bare shoulder. It sent shivers through me.

"If you want to be sworn in, you'll stop that right now. Otherwise, you're going to be late and miss the ceremony."

"You're right," he said and backed up, eyeing himself in the mirror, making funny faces with his jaw. "Did I miss a spot shaving?"

Then his phone dinged. He glanced down.

"Our car is here."

The ceremony was confusing and a total whirlwind with Secret Service guys marching us around from room to room and then out to our car when it was all over.

As soon as we stepped back into the hotel room, I flopped on the bed.

Anthony laughed. He was over at the room service cart popping the cork on a bottle of Champagne.

"Is your life always this hectic?" I asked. "I feel like every second I spend with you takes place at lightning speed."

He didn't answer. He just handed me a glass of Champagne.

I sat up and sipped it. I'd already had a few drinks at the swearing in reception so I was feeling a little tipsy.

"I'm not complaining," I said.

"Good."

He took off his tie and then grabbed me by my wrists, holding them over my head and tying them together with the silky material.

I arched an eyebrow.

"I like where this is going," I said.

"Just wait."

34

Anthony was better in bed than I'd even imagined.

"Well, that was worth the wait," I said in the morning when he opened his eyes to find me propped up on one elbow watching him.

"Of course it was," he said. "Anticipation always makes things better."

I frowned. "I wouldn't go that far."

He laughed.

I smiled. "I think my favorite thing about you is your laugh."

He scowled. "Obviously, it wasn't worth the wait if that's your favorite thing about me. Get over here so I can change your mind."

"I have to go," I said, rolling out of his grasp. "The driver is already downstairs ready to take me to the airport. His call was what woke me up. It's two in the afternoon, you know."

"Damn," Anthony said. "Why don't you cancel your ticket? Fly back with me this weekend"

"I can't. I have a stupid board meeting to attend tomorrow morning. Early."

After I dressed, I gave him a long deep kiss. He was scrambling to put his pants on.

"I'm escorting you to the airport."

"I'm good," I said. Before he could answer, I'd grabbed my duffel bag and was gone.

When I stepped off the plane in San Francisco, I was exhausted and couldn't wait to get home. But I realized I hadn't called my regular driver, Tony. I glanced at the time.

It was past midnight. Flying commercial meant I had a hell of a layover in Chicago because of the weather. I wasn't going to bug Tony this late. I'd find a cab.

I was yawning as I walked past security gates and into the main airport so at first I didn't see him sitting there.

Dante.

He wore a black suit and held up a huge white poster board.

I read it and felt tears slipping down my cheeks.

"GIA SANTELLA. I'M AN ASS. I LOVE YOU. PLEASE FORGIVE ME."

I dropped my duffel bag and wrapped him in a big hug.

"Of course I forgive you, you goof. You're *famiglia*. You are my true family whether you like it or not forever and ever."

I whispered the words in his ear.

He squeezed me even tighter.

We pulled back and he put his arm around me.

"Let's go, paesana. Your car awaits."

I was still yawning and sleepily following him when he led me out to the curb. The surprises weren't over.

I nearly fell to my knees when I saw who was waiting, leaning up against the black car with her arms crossed across her chest.

Rose.

I ran over and hugged her like my life depended on it.

"What are you doing here?"

We caught up for a few minutes and all three of us had tears streaming down our faces.

Finally, Dante cleared his throat.

"It's late. Let's head home."

The three of us crawled into the backseat of the car. I leaned my head on Dante's shoulder and Rose leaned her head on mine.

We left the airport and headed north into the city. San Francisco was lit up in all her glory and there was a haze of orange clouds above her and as I took it all in and squeezed both Dante and Rose's hands, I'd never in my life felt happier to be home.

The story continues in *Deadly Lies*, the next Gia Santella Thriller. Head to the next page for a sneak peek or order today by clicking the link or scanning the QR code below!
www.amazon.com/B09D8VPQJT

Stay up to date with Kristi Belcamino's new releases by clicking the link or scanning the QR code below!
(You'll receive a **free** copy of *First Vengeance: A Gia Santella Prequel!*)
https://liquidmind.media/kristi-belcamino-newsletter-signup-1-first-vengeance/

Did you enjoy *Deadly Justice*? Click the link or scan the QR code below to let us know your thoughts!
www.amazon.com/B08VRF3GNT

DEADLY LIES CHAPTER ONE

I leaned my back against the wall and watched Rose through the crowded room.

She was perched on the edge of an emerald green velvet ottoman listening intently to another young woman speak.

Darling's massive and opulent living room was filled with people holding drinks and laughing and talking. The soft sounds of Marvin Gaye could barely be heard under the chatter. The low lights infused faces with a soft glow. A glittering chandelier in the center of the room was turned down low.

The party spilled out of the room and through the French doors onto the patio. Just beyond, the pool was lit up, turquoise blue and shimmering.

Everyone was dressed up except Rose.

Even me. Dante had ordered me to wear my knee-length leather dress with the cap sleeves. It hugged my curves without showing any flesh. I didn't argue. I loved butter soft leather. Unlike some of the dresses he made me wear, this one was comfortable and didn't feel all that different from wearing my beloved leather pants and a worn, soft T-shirt.

When I told Rose I'd be dressing up for the party, she looked at me without answering.

Later, she came out of her guest room at Darling's wearing a black tank top and charcoal gray cargo pants. Her long black hair fell down her back in a shiny sheet. Her huge black eyes and naturally red lips didn't need any makeup. Her dark skin was flawless.

"You look nice," she said about my dress.

I just walked up and hugged her. I was trying not to cry.

The party was her goodbye party.

I'd had her for a month. Four long, glorious weeks of catching up.

We'd spent some of it talking about her father.

We cried together remembering Nico and how we'd lost him to Alzheimer's long before we'd lost him to death.

More than a few nights were spent curled up on the couch in my hotel suite watching movies. Mostly, she sat in the living room and read all day. I asked her several times if she wanted to go out, but she would shake her head no.

Dante was with us the first two weeks. He and I had been busy with hotel business. We'd finally renovated the hotel the way we wanted to. Dante launched the re-opening of the restaurant and was planning to come back next month for a larger party.

Wayne, his husband, had flown up, and we'd spent a few nights at restaurants in North Beach, eating Italian food and drinking wine and talking late into the night until the managers kicked us out.

My heart was full. It had been a long time since I'd felt this much peace and love in my life.

But now Rose was leaving me again.

She missed her boyfriend. She missed her dog.

She missed her life without me.

I'd tried to argue, but she just looked at me and said, "There's someone out there killing young girls. What would you do?"

I gave her a slow nod.

I had been raised in a fairly normal house and had a fairly normal childhood. And yet, I still had blood on my hands.

Rose had been raised with murder and violence and death as a constant companion.

She'd only found peace once she'd accepted that she was born to be a killer.

I could never understand. I could only love her as she was and be there for her in every possible way.

She had not needed me for years.

But one night in the hotel room, she had wept about the lives she had taken and the role she felt she needed to play in life.

"You don't have to live this way," I told her. "You can have a normal life."

But even as I said it, we both knew it was a lie.

Now, watching her from across the room, I loved how she didn't feel the need to fit in. And the irony was, that even without makeup or fancy clothes, she was easily the most striking woman in the room. And Darling had some really beautiful friends with exquisite taste. Their makeup, hair, clothing and accessories were always perfect. I'd never seen one of Darling's tribe of friends dressed casually.

It was the way Rose held herself. So poised and confident for someone so young.

She was wise beyond her years.

I sat in the corner and must've given off a vibe because everyone let me be.

Or probably, more likely, Darling had told everyone to give me space.

She knew my heart was breaking.

At one point I walked over and joined Rose, scooting onto the edge of the ottoman.

Darling's two fancy-ass, expensive-as-fuck dogs were on the couch on either side of the woman Rose had been talking to.

She was stroking one's fur absentmindedly. The other had its head on her lap. So cute.

"I'm Gia," I said to her.

"Clara," the young woman said. Her infectious smile lit up her face, and she had striking green eyes against dark skin.

"You guys have been deep in conversation all night," I said. "Looked intense."

They both laughed.

"We were actually talking about rescue dogs," Clara said and reached over to scratch one of the dog's heads. "I'm studying law and working as a paralegal, so I'm not home enough to have one yet, but I'm counting the days until I can get my own dog."

Darling came over.

"I see you've met my grandniece, Clara," she said, pulling up a chair. "She's going to do big things. Change this country."

The young woman gave a nervous laugh and said, "If only all of us could live up to how Darling sees us; the world would be a better place."

"Honey, you are going to change the world. I have no doubt." Darling turned to me. "Valedictorian of her class."

I nodded, impressed.

Another woman nearby reached over and plucked a piece of cheese off a platter on the table by us.

"I love this cheese!" she said.

"Me too," Darling said.

"It is stinky though," the woman said.

People laughed.

"This is Kat," Darling said and introduced us.

"I have a funny story about stinky cheese," Kat said.

She told us that a divorcing couple was arguing over who should get the house. The husband had more money, and so he was able to force the woman out. Shortly after the wife moved out the man noticed an awful smell. He searched high and low for the source of the smell and couldn't find it. He brought in professionals and they were at a loss. Finally, he decided to sell the house because he just couldn't hack the smell anymore. All the people who came to look at it left, horrified because of the smell. Finally, his real estate agent told him he was just going to have to sell the house at a loss. He agreed.

As soon as the house was reduced in price, a real estate agent called up, and said she'd buy the house sight unseen.

"I have to disclose that there's a major odor issue," the husband's agent said.

"That's fine. Just draw up the paperwork. I don't want a long escrow."

A month later the wife moved into the house she'd just bought. The first thing she did was take down the circular curtain rods and throw them in the trash. She'd unscrewed the decorative ends and stuffed smelly cheese inside.

Everyone listening to the story burst into laughter, Clara especially. Her laughter was infectious.

Right after, her phone chirped. She looked down and frowned, then stood. "Excuse me for a second."

As she walked off toward the patio, I gave Darling a look.

She rolled her eyes. "She's the smartest person I know except when it comes to the men in her life."

I shot a look at Rose.

"What? Don't look at me. Damon and I are taking a break."

"You're leaving to go see him in the morning."

She scoffed. "Just to get my dog back."

But I was worried. I knew they truly loved each other, but I didn't think they were good for one another. I reminded myself that it was none of my business.

Darling was watching Clara as she paced out by the pool.

"Excuse me," she finally said and got up.

Rose yawned.

"You can go to bed," I said. "Darling will understand. You have an early start."

"You sure?"

I smiled. "Go on. I'll tell her you've gone to bed. Sneak out now."

She smiled and headed toward the back hall of the bedrooms.

My heart hurt as I watched her go.

By this time tomorrow, she'd be back in Florida.

I saw Darling out by the pool talking to Clara. Then a third woman joined them.

She was older, maybe in her early forties. She looked like an older version of Clara. I assumed it must be her mom. She didn't look happy.

Clara shrugged and gestured toward her phone.

Then the three came back in.

"Rose said to say goodbye. I sent her to bed. She has to be up at four to head back to the city for her flight."

Darling nodded. "Clara has to leave now anyway."

"Everything okay?" I asked.

"It's a long story," the woman said and smiled.

"A long story that has nothing to do with you," her mother quipped.

"I'm Gia," I said and stuck out my hand.

"Alisha Parks." Her grip was firm and her smile genuine. "I've heard so much about you."

I immediately recognized her name. She was a longtime friend and sorority sister of Darling's.

"Same," I said. "I can't believe we haven't met before now."

"I think we were both out of the country at different times," she said.

I remembered Darling had mentioned that Alisha Park's husband was a diplomat in Singapore.

"Are you living back in the States now or just on a visit?"

"Home for good," she said. "Thank god. I missed my tribe."

Darling nodded. "Mmmhmm. Wasn't the same without Alisha around."

It wasn't the first time I envied Darling's close knit group of friends.

I had my close friends: Dante, Darling, and Danny. (Obviously, you had to have a name that starts with a "D" to be my friend. Lol.)

But they were not just friends; they were family.

I'd never had a big group of close girlfriends.

I wasn't sure why. Maybe because I wasn't into shopping and gossip and soccer vans.

Yeah, that was probably it.

Darling was speaking quietly to people, and I noticed groups were leaving. She must have told them the party was over.

I went up to her. "I'm sneaking off now. Thank you."

"I'll see you in the morning."

"You don't have to get up to see us off."

She gave me a sideways irritated look.

"Fine," I said.

I learned a long time ago to never argue with that woman.

DEADLY LIES CHAPTER TWO

Not only was Darling up early, but she was dressed to the nines —as always—and had breakfast waiting for us.

Rose had dark circles under her eyes and was quiet, sipping her black coffee and nibbling on a cinnamon cardamom scone Darling had baked.

Then it was time to go.

Rose fell into Darling's large embrace and stayed there a long time. Darling was patting her back and making eyes at me over the top of her head. I wasn't sure what she was trying to convey, but she leaned down and said into Rose's ear, "Don't you ever forget Miss Rose that you have two mamas here in the Bay Area—me and Gia. We love you like you are our own flesh and blood, and don't you ever forget it!"

Darling's voice was soft but fierce.

Rose nodded her head and pulled back.

Without looking at me, she headed straight to the front door.

I went over and kissed Darling's cheek. "Thanks, Darling."

Darling put her hands on her hips. "We're family."

"I know."

"Don't you spend a second worrying about that girl. I don't."

"You don't?"

"Nuh uh. She is stronger than the two of us put together—physically, emotionally, and mentally."

I sighed. "I hope you're right."

Darling lifted one eyebrow and I laughed.

Darling was always right.

I'd taken my newest car—a Maserati SUV—up to Darling's house in Mill Valley in the Marin headlands.

I didn't want my driver, Tony, to drive this far this early in the morning.

He was an ex-convict with a gold tooth and gold heart.

I'd bought the SUV a few weeks before when Rose came to town so I had something to drive to show her around and take her places. During her stay, we'd taken short weekend getaways. Even though my hotel room was a suite, it felt small for the two of us. We'd gone to Fort Bragg up the coast for a few days, to Calistoga to visit Dante while he was in town checking on his restaurants, and to Sacramento to tour the capitol.

I'd offered the car to Rose to use while she was there, but she had zero interest in leaving the room. It was only because of my insistence that we take the small trips that we left at all.

I was worried about her. I knew she was still grieving the loss of her father. Hell, I was still grieving his loss and always would be. But this was something else. She seemed distracted.

Now, in the car, I reached over and squeezed her hand.

"You okay?"

She smiled, and it lit up her face.

"Yeah. I'm excited to see Damon and Dylan."

I returned her smile.

"I'm so glad."

Then her smile disappeared.

"Gia, I don't want you to worry about me."

I took a deep breath and nodded. "I'm going to try my best. It would help if you could maybe keep in touch a bit more..."

She winced.

Fuck. I wasn't asking that much.

"I will when I can."

"Okay," I said.

But she wasn't done yet.

"Damon and I are going to be off the grid."

I waited.

"I bought a sailboat, and we're heading toward the Bermuda Triangle. That's where I think the person working with the Sultan is living," she said. "We're going to come in the back door."

I nodded.

The Sultan had been a cult leader who brainwashed young girls into being sex slaves. He sacrificed several of them. And endlessly taunted Rose.

It was only when she was forced with the decision of whether or not to kill him that he revealed he was her own brother.

And she killed him anyway.

I knew her new adventure was dangerous, but there was nothing I could say to stop her.

At the airport, I dropped her off at the curb. I got out and hugged her tightly.

"I love you, Gia," she said and gave me a smile that melted my heart.

"I love you, sweet girl."

It was what her father had always called her.

She smiled and walked away without answering.

Back at the hotel, my suite felt empty without Rose and her things, but I dove into some hotel business I'd put off during her visit, and before I realized it, the sky out my window had turned a dark blue.

I ordered a salad and fish from room service. I had been focusing on eating healthy and exercising for the past month while Rose was there.

I hadn't really had alcohol since Anthony came to town and took us all out to dinner.

He was back in Washington, DC now in his new role as senator.

He promised to split his time between there and here, but for the first legislative session, he said he needed to be there to learn the ropes.

I hated to admit that I missed him. But he said he would be back in town this weekend.

I decided to forego the red wine and save it for dinner with him.

My dinner was amazing—Dante luring the city's top chef to our restaurant not only benefited the hotel; it benefited me personally. After I ate, I curled up on my couch and tried to watch a Spanish film that had been lauded at the Cannes film festival.

But I couldn't concentrate and turned it off.

Finally, the loneliness I'd been keeping at bay hit me hard.

My willpower was gone.

I ordered a pack of Dunhill blue cigarettes and two bourbons from room service—two items that I made sure the hotel stocked after Dante and I bought it.

I told room service to leave everything in my private hallway and to text me when they'd been delivered.

I was wearing only a tight tank top and my underwear and didn't feel like getting dressed just to answer the door.

A wave of overwhelming sadness overcame me.

I swallowed. It was a life I'd chosen.

I'd made a decision to live this life. It didn't mean that I'd always be alone. I had friends who were more precious than any blood relatives.

And I had two amazing men in my life who let me be me.

But still I found myself alone more often than not.

And so I was weak. I would tamp down the loneliness in ways I'd always done.

I wouldn't spend every last dime or sleep with every cute boy, but I would turn to vices that never did me any good—nicotine and alcohol.

Thinking this, I called room service back and told them to bring me an entire bottle of bourbon and a bucket of ice.

A few minutes later, I'd made myself a drink and was out on my deck wrapped in a blanket.

I stayed there a long time, drinking and smoking and watching the fog roll in under the Golden Gate Bridge.

Are you loving *Deadly Lies*? Scan the QR code below to order your copy today!

ALSO BY KRISTI BELCAMINO

Enjoying Kristi Belcamino? Scan the code below to see her Amazon Author page!

Gia Santella Crime Thriller Series

Vendetta

Vigilante

Vengeance

Black Widow

Day of the Dead

Border Line

Night Fall

Stone Cold

Cold as Death

Cold Blooded

Dark Shadows

Dark Vengeance

Dark Justice

Deadly Justice

Deadly Lies

Additional books in series:

Taste of Vengeance

Lone Raven

Vigilante Crime Series

Blood & Roses

Blood & Fire

Blood & Bone

Blood & Tears

Queen of Spades Thrillers

Queen of Spades

The One-Eyed Jack

The Suicide King

The Ace of Clubs

The Joker

The Wild Card

High Stakes

Poker Face

Standalone Novels

Coming For You

Sanctuary City

The Girl in the River

Buried Secrets

Dead Wrong (Young Adult Mystery)

Gabriella Giovanni Mystery Series

Blessed are the Dead

Blessed are the Meek

Blessed are Those Who Weep

Blessed are Those Who Mourn

Blessed are the Peacemakers

Blessed are the Merciful

Nonfiction

Letters from a Serial Killer

ALSO BY WITHOUT WARRANT

More Thriller Series from Without Warrant Authors

Dana Gray Mysteries by C.J. Cross

Girl Left Behind

Girl on the Hill

Girl in the Grave

The Kenzie Gilmore Series by Biba Pearce

Afterburn

Dead Heat

Heatwave

Burnout

Deep Heat

Fever Pitch

Storm Surge (Coming Soon)

Willow Grace FBI Thrillers by Anya Mora

Shadow of Grace

Condition of Grace (Coming Soon)

Gia Santella Crime Thriller Series by Kristi Belcamino

Vendetta

Vigilante

Vengeance

Black Widow

Day of the Dead

Border Line

Night Fall

Stone Cold

Cold as Death

Cold Blooded

Dark Shadows

Dark Vengeance

Dark Justice

Deadly Justice

Deadly Lies

Vigilante Crime Series by Kristi Belcamino

Blood & Roses

Blood & Fire

Blood & Bone

Blood & Tears

Queen of Spades Thrillers by Kristi Belcamino

Queen of Spades

The One-Eyed Jack

The Suicide King

The Ace of Clubs

The Joker

The Wild Card

High Stakes

Poker Face

AUTHOR'S NOTE

When I was 16, I read Jackie Collins' book, *Lucky*, and it rocked my world. For the first time in my prolific reading life (yes, I was the kid holed up in my room reading as many books as I could as often as I could), I met a character who was not only Italian-American like me, but a strong, powerful, and successful badass woman who didn't take crap from anybody and loved to have sex!

Although I had dreamed of being a writer, it never seemed like a realistic dream and my attempts at writing seemed pitiful. So I studied journalism and became a reporter—it was a way to be a writer and have a steady paycheck.

It was only when I was in my forties that I got the guts to write a book. And it was a few years after that I was brave enough to write the character I really wanted to write—Gia Santella.

She's not Lucky Santangelo, of course. I mean, nobody could be as cool as Lucky is, but I like to think that maybe Gia and Lucky would have been friends.

Gia is my alter ego. The woman who does and says things I

never could or would, but whom I admire and would love to be friends with.

If you like her, I'm pretty sure we'd be the best of friends in real life!

x Kristi

ABOUT THE AUTHOR

Kristi Belcamino is a USA Today bestseller, an Agatha, Anthony, Barry & Macavity finalist, and an Italian Mama who bakes a tasty biscotti.

Her books feature strong, kickass, independent women facing unspeakable evil in order to seek justice for those unable to do so themselves.

In her former life, as an award-winning crime reporter at newspapers in California, she flew over Big Sur in an FA-18 jet with the Blue Angels, raced a Dodge Viper at Laguna Seca, attended barbecues at the morgue, and conversed with serial killers.

During her decade covering crime, Belcamino wrote and reported about many high-profile cases including the Laci Peterson murder and Chandra Levy disappearance. She has appeared on *Inside Edition* and local television shows. She now writes fiction and works part-time as a reporter covering the police beat for the St. Paul *Pioneer Press*.

Her work has appeared in such prominent publications as *Salon*, the *Miami Herald*, *San Jose Mercury News,* and *Chicago Tribune*.

facebook.com/kristibelcaminowriter
instagram.com/kristibelcaminobooks
tiktok.com/@kristibelcaminobooks

Printed in the USA
CPSIA information can be obtained
at www.ICGtesting.com
LVHW021127310524
781581LV00015B/1113